S·H·A·R·K G·I·R·L

S·H·A·R·K G·I·R·L

KELLY BINGHAM

CANDLEWICK PRESS
CAMBRIDGE, MASSACHUSETTS

First edition 2007

Library of Congress Cataloging-in-Publication Data
Bingham, Kelly L., date.
Shark girl / Kelly Bingham. —1st ed.
p.   cm.
Summary: After a shark attack causes the amputation of her right arm, fifteen-year-old
Jane, an aspiring artist, struggles to come to terms with her loss and the changes it imposes
on her day-to-day life and her plans for the future.
ISBN 978-0-7636-3207-6
[1. Amputees—Fiction. 2. Artists—Fiction. 3. People with disabilities—Fiction.
4. Self-acceptance—Fiction. 5. Interpersonal relations—Fiction. 6. Novels in verse.]
I. Title.
PZ7.5.B56Sha 2007
[Fic]—dc22   2006049120

4   6   8   10   9   7   5

Printed in the United States of America

This book was typeset in Granjon.

Candlewick Press
2067 Massachusetts Avenue
Cambridge, Massachusetts 02140

visit us at www.candlewick.com

For my parents, and for Sam and Benny,
with much love

CONTENTS

Part • One
1

Part • Two
85

Part • Three
195

Ghost

Sometimes
I can still feel my right hand,
like a best friend;
weighted,
warm.

Sometimes
Mom looks for a tissue
or the book
lying among my covers
and I reach for it,
then I remember
I cannot reach with that hand
ever again.

Sometimes
a prickle crawls across my cheek,
and that right hand tries to
rise from the grave,
moved to scratch.
The fingers, palm,
wrist, and arm
that I remember
don't know enough
to know
peace.

O · N · E

I Remember

I remember
the first time,
and the last time,
I wore my
pink bikini.
Michael teased me.
He said,
"Why don't you give that thing to someone who can fill it out?"
A driver's license in his wallet,
so high on freedom,
he was more obnoxious than usual.
I threw the towels at him.
Mom hefted him the cooler.

We filled up the trunk,
Michael slid behind the wheel,
Mom pasted sunscreen around her ears.
The sun was so bright that day.
As we pulled out of the driveway,
I reached for the beach bag
and slipped my sketchbook inside.

A fifteen-year-old girl was attacked by a shark at Point Dume State Beach yesterday afternoon. The girl was swimming approximately four yards from shore in waters four to five feet deep when the shark attacked.

"I was just down the shore from her," one witness said. "Everything was fine, then all of a sudden I heard people screaming. Everyone started running out of the water. It was crazy. I looked, and saw people pointing. I saw the girl trying to swim."

Another witness described the scene: "I saw her out there, kind of going under, then back up again. There was all this blood. They got her out of there and laid her on the sand, and I thought she was dead, there was just so much blood coming out of her. Her arm was barely attached to her body. It was terrifying."

The girl's brother is credited with saving her life. After pulling her from the water, he used a string to tie off the injured limb and slow blood loss.

Frightened beachgoers watched as paramedics arrived. The girl was transported to UCLA hospital, where she is listed in critical condition. Doctors had to amputate her right arm due to injuries inflicted by the shark.

"She is lucky to be alive," Dr. Andrew Kim, head of orthopedic surgery, reports. "She is in a coma due to blood loss. The next forty-eight hours are critical. We have no way of knowing yet if she sustained brain damage from the massive blood loss."

Authorities closed down the beach and it remains closed today, but a spokesman said it will probably open again tomorrow. The Coast Guard has found no evidence of the shark in patrolling the area since yesterday.

Home Movies

I didn't think
things could get much worse
when the doctors told me,
their voices penetrating
some faraway cloud
I'd been inhaling,
"Jane, we've had to amputate.
Your right arm, Jane.
Above the elbow."
I didn't think things could get worse.
But then I was in a coma for
the first ten days.

"There's video."
Michael gives it to me straight.
"Some person on the beach.
He was taping his kids and then . . ."

He stares at his palms.

"The guy is a bastard."

Details come
from everyone else.

"They blurred out the really bad parts,"
Mom says, her eyes wet.

"I haven't seen it. I hope I never do.
The news finally stopped playing it
about a week after you—
after it happened."

The nurse says,
"Don't watch it, if it comes up again.
Just try and put that day behind you."

Hot tears
slide down into my ears.
Rage boils
in me so wild,
it almost

swallows my fear.

Holding

I hold on to Mom's hand with my left one now.
Her hand is warm and soft.
I feel so hot, so thirsty, all the time.
She pours me water.

I think, constantly, about my art—my life.
Why did this happen? Why me?
I was supposed to be an artist.
Has there been a mistake? Can it be fixed?
How can I live without drawing?
What am I supposed to do now?
These are my questions,
running like hamsters on wheels,
but I ask,
"Who's covering for you at school?"

Mom teaches English at USC.
"They found a substitute," she says,
and squeezes my fingers. "Don't worry about it.
Your grandparents are coming Friday;
they can help out when I go back."

Our hands separate when the
phone rings. Rachel, my best friend,
checking in. All my other friends,
calling to see if they can come visit.
I can't even talk to them.

I feel like words
might force my stomach to come up.
Mom takes over.

"If you could wait a few more days,
that would be best," she tells
everyone who calls.

Mom goes for coffee
while my blood pressure is taken,
my temperature charted,
my bandages rewrapped.

Though I'm dozing off when she returns,
I'm aware of her hand
slipping back over mine.
Warm, and soft.

Phone Call, July 3

Jane? How are you?

Hi, Aunt Karen. I'm fine.

No you're not. You're not fine at all. I'm sorry—that was a dumb question.

It's okay.

Lord, it's good to hear your voice. We haven't slept a minute, waiting for you to come out of that coma. We're coming out next week to see you. You know we could hardly stand waiting, but your uncle just had his knee surgery.

I know.

You sound strong. Are they taking care of you in that hospital?

Yes.

Are you in pain? Your mother said you were having some pain.

It's not too bad today. It comes and goes.

Oh, Jane. I'm just . . . I . . .

It's okay.

Will you listen to her? (Voice grows distant.) She's telling me it's okay, Ben. Jane, you don't have to be brave for me.

Okay.

Hold on, your uncle Ben wants to talk to you. He's about to rip the phone out of my hand.

Janie?

Hi, Uncle Ben. How's your knee?

Forget the damned knee. I love you, honey, and you're going to be okay. Whatever happens, at least you're alive. We thought we were going to lose you, you know. We just thank God you're going to recover.

Yeah.

I mean it. It will be okay. I know it looks rough now, but you are . . .

Strong?

Hell, yes. Strong. All right, here's Karen. Love you. Take care, now, all right? Listen to the doctors. We'll be out next week.

Okay.

I'm here, Jane.

I have to go. It's time for my physical therapy.

Eat right, Jane. And take your time with everything. Listen to the doctors.

All right.

And don't watch too much . . . uh, don't watch TV.

Have you seen the video?

I have, and we don't even need to discuss it.

Is it . . .

I love you, and I'll call you tomorrow.

Michael

I remember
spreading out the towels.
Michael wanted the yellow one.
It was biggest.

"Yeah, you need it for your fat head,"
I told him.
Michael dug into the cooler,
tossed a river of ice at me.
"Have a shower, Jane the pain."

There were four girls,
all from Michael's class,
stretched out on their bellies.

Michael sat on the yellow towel,
pretending to read a magazine.
He watched the girl in the green suit.
I laughed at him
as I stood to go.

Mom said,
"Michael, why don't you go in with Jane?
It looks a little choppy today."

"I don't need him to come with me,"
I said.

But I was kind of hoping he would come.
It was always more fun
with Michael along.
But
he was too busy
not watching
the girl.

Nerves

"When will that pain stop?"
Mom asks the doctor
as he squeezes my flesh,
making sure circulation is healthy.
"She keeps saying she feels pain,
in the end there,
and sometimes cold. Right, Jane?"

"Yes." I want to tell her to let *me* talk,
but the doctor is giving her a look,
and turning away from us both.
"This is not an exact science," he says,
stabbing his pen into his shirt pocket.
"Phantom pain is part of the fallout
of amputation. It may last a few weeks.
It may last a person's lifetime."

Why does he say "a person's"?
Me. We're talking about me.

Mom makes annoyed sounds when he leaves,
more when the nurse brings breakfast
twenty minutes late,
more when the second-shift nurse
delivers medication and doesn't know
what the blue pill is for.
"Nobody tells us anything," Mom says.

Michael, who has dropped in for dinner,
stretches lazily. "What do you expect?
It's a hospital.
Everyone's too busy to take *care* of people."
"It's not a joke!" Mom snaps.
"Damn it, *why* can't you be more help?"

The shock on Michael's face
is a mirror of her own
and probably mine, too.
The words hang in the air,
long after Michael has left.

I Wonder

Why didn't that man
put down his camera
and help me?

And why, why, why
did he give that video
to the news?

Jane Arrowood, the teenage girl attacked by a shark last month, is reported to be in stable condition. The fifteen-year-old is a resident of Santa Clarita and attends Mountain Ridge High School, where she will be a junior this fall.

"She is doing well, has suffered no brain damage, and will be going home soon," her surgeon, Dr. Andrew Kim, reports. "She is very, very lucky."

The young beachgoer lost her right arm in the attack, which happened mid-morning at a crowded beach. The attack was caught on tape and has gained widespread attention.

Ms. Arrowood was a well-known artist at Mountain Ridge, having won state art competitions the last two years in a row, and last year claiming top prize in the West Coast Wings Competition, a contest held annually that selects the best work of art from state champions of California, Oregon, Washington, and Nevada.

There is no word yet on her exact date of release.

Pity Bears

"Mail call!"
Lindsey, my nurse,
carries in the day's stack of white envelopes,
with one red one, like a spot of blood,
peeking out of the pale pile.
"No," I groan.

"Wow, the stack is smaller today,"
Michael observes. "Maybe
your fifteen minutes is up."
I laugh a little, though it's not funny.
Mom frowns at our bad manners.

"And one more thing," Lindsey adds.
From her pocket, she whips out a tiny white bear
with a pink heart in its stuffed paws.
"This one arrived today."

Tubes spiral around my bed,
some of them enter my body.
The pain medication leaves me floating,
but not high enough to shut out the Pity Bears.

That's what I call them,
all the teddy bears strangers send me.
And the flowers.
The smell was suffocating. I had to

beg Michael to deliver them to the other rooms.
I give the bears to the younger kids on the hall.
"Like it or not, you're a celebrity,"
Lindsey says.
She puts her cool hand on my cheek,
then my forehead.
"People care. They want you to know that."

I say, "But I don't want this, any of it."
Mom gets a flash in her eye
and snaps,

"Jane, for God's sake, just appreciate it.
People are trying to help,
not embarrass you."

So I shut up,
because who wants to fight
while lying in a hospital bed?
Besides,
mail call is the highlight of Mom's day.

Each day, she and Lindsey rip open the cards,
turn to me with eager smiles,
read to me like I'm a baby.
"Doesn't that make you feel better?" Mom asks,
holding up a rainbow drawing some child made.

Michael is the only one who understands,
pretending to gag when Mom isn't looking.
This is pity,
pure and simple.
People have watched that damned video
and been shocked into wanting to do something—
something for That Poor Girl.
Shark Girl.

Me.

A Letter from Mary, Age 7

Dear Jane,

I saw the pictures on TV. Mom says you lost your arm. Your right one. The doctors cut my arm off, too. I had cancer. After they cut it off, I got all better. Are you all better now? I have a new arm. I named her Patty. I can play at the park with all my friends like I used to. I am on the soccer team. Patty helps me do a lot of things.

After I was all better, my mom and dad and I had a funeral for my arm. We played music and made a grave and I put flowers from our garden on the grave. It was nice. My real arm was not in the grave. The doctors threw it away already. But we pretended. Maybe you should have a pretend funeral, too. So you can say good-bye.

My mom wrote this letter for me. But I can write by myself.

Love,
Mary

Corny

It sounds clichéd.
But at times like this,
I miss my dad.
I mean,
I don't remember him—
he died of cancer when I was three.
Pictures
are all that's left.
My favorite one is us
sitting on a bench, eating ice cream.
Our knees are knobby the same way,
we're both grinning like hyenas,
he's pointing at the camera.

I haven't had a dad in twelve years.
Most of the time,
that's okay.
But today,
right now,
I'd like a hug.
From him.

Permission

I wasn't sure about having a man
be my therapist.
Or shrink, as Rachel calls him.
But he was assigned by the hospital.
That first day
when Mel walked into my room,
with his gray mustache,
and his loud tie,
my body tightened.
That whole long hour,
more silence than words.

Now our sessions fly by.
"Big picture," Mel tells me.
He says this when I'm telling him
how many things I have to relearn
or how fear keeps me from breathing right.
"Big picture, Jane," he says.
"You could have died.
Instead, you are here. You have time to find out why.
You have your whole life to discover
and rebuild."

I know what he's thinking.
He's thinking about the terminally ill kids
upstairs. Bald heads and sad eyes
and weeping parents—

that's *real* tragedy.
My problem
must not seem like much of a problem
to them.
The really sick kids should get the balloons,
cards, and letters from all over.
Not me.

"It's in our nature . . . our culture, really,"
Mel says, "to think that when we are depressed,
we need to cheer ourselves up right away.
That's not always healthy."
He faces me with gray eyes and a shiny spot
on his balding head.
It's like he knows my thoughts and doesn't judge.
"You have lost your right arm.
That is a tremendous, heartbreaking loss.
You have every right to be depressed.
Don't fight it. Allow yourself to feel as bad as you want.
The sooner you do this,
the sooner you will be able to move on."

My tears are
loud
and ugly
and awful.
They keep tumbling and tearing,

from deep inside somewhere,
somewhere
down
dark
and black.
When will they stop?

Lies

Grandma and Grandpa arrived today.
Michael picked them up at the airport.
They stepped into my tiny white room,
Grandpa looking terrified,
Grandma simmering with tears.

"Jane!" they blurted, and "Katherine!" to Mom,
and there were exclamations all around,
the smell of Grandpa's cinnamon gum,
and Grandma sweeping my hair behind my ears.
"You look beautiful," she said.

"She's getting fitted for her prosthesis next month,"
Mom said. They all stood around the foot of my bed,
breathing in the monitors and bandages,
the smell of antiseptic.
Grandma dabbed her eyes with a tissue.
"Well, they better treat her right. Sometimes
hospital staff can be rather callous."
She used to be an ER nurse, so she knows.

"The nurses here are nice," I say. "Mostly."
Grandma nods triumphantly. "Uh-huh. *Mostly*.
If anyone gives you trouble, you tell them—"
"Mom, they're fine. They're all fine," Mom says.
Grandpa pats my leg. "It sure is good to see you, Janie."
He jingles coins in his pockets;

Gram clutches her purse straps;
they stare unseeingly at the cards lined up
on the windowsill
as Mom fills them in on my progress.
"Doesn't she look good? She's doing great—
she's eating, getting her physical therapy,
improving each day,
and she's handling all this so well."
Grandma and Grandpa finally swallow
and unstick themselves, finding two chairs,
relaxing into them, and sighing.

"She'll be going home in no time,"
Mom adds. "And then things
will be a lot better."

She has convinced herself.
So I keep quiet. But really.

Better?

Six Days After

Six days after waking from my coma,
I am allowed to have my best friend, Rachel, visit.
I put on a clean gown and brush my hair—
nervous. Ready to get that first look over with.

"Hi," she says, stepping into the room,
clutching a red rose. "I brought you a—"
she stares at the day's delivery of flowers.
"Whoa."
Michael and I laugh;
even Mom smiles.
The ice is broken, and Rachel sits on my bed,
filling me in on what's been going on in the world
since June 21.

"Come on, Mike, let's get some lunch," Mom says,
and Michael pinches my foot as he passes the bed.

There's a long pause while Rachel just sits
and stares at my short arm in its hard, rounded cast.
"I can't believe it, Jane."
"Me either." We both contemplate the thing.
"You're going to draw again," Rachel says suddenly.
"People have stuff happen and they learn to get along
with their other hand just as well."

"Rachel . . ."
"I mean it. I mean . . .
I don't know what to say."

"You don't have to say anything," I tell her,
my throat suddenly closing and tears rising
to the surface. "I wish everyone would
either say what they think
or say nothing.
Everybody that comes by, everyone who calls . . .
I end up having to tell them it's okay.
I'm tired of saying it's okay."

Rachel is quiet for a moment. "It's not okay.
I think, if it were me, I'd go crazy."

Simple words that hurt
because they are the words I would say
if *she* were lying in this bed.
Why me? Why?

Friday Afternoon

Michael?

Hmm?

Have you seen the . . . the video of . . .

No.

Michael.

What? You want some more water? Do you need to sit up?

Where did you get the belt?

What belt?

The thing you used to tie off my arm. To stop the bleeding.

I used the cord from my swimsuit.

That was fast thinking.

Somebody had to do something.

Did you see the shark, Michael? I mean, what did you see?

I saw you floundering around, and I saw a thing, a shape.

Then there was just a lot of . . .

Blood.

Well. Yeah.

Weren't you afraid?

Of course I was. I thought you were dead.

No, I mean, weren't you afraid that the shark would get you, too? When you swam out to get me?

No. I just knew I had to get you fast.

The person who videotaped . . .

I'm sure it was a coincidence that they had the thing on. But they could have helped, huh?

Yeah.

Hope they're proud of themselves.

Michael.

What?

Thanks. For saving my life.

Pain

Sawing
with a rusty,
wobbly saw.

Tingling—
a wet finger
in an electric socket,
permanently.

Throbbing.
The skin that is gone
stretched tight,
glove squashing tight
over tender bones
that are no longer there.

Ache—
as though my arm is still here,
and bent backward,
twisted, taut, spiraling down deep
ache.

Always.

Dreams

I walk along,
sidewalk hot;
a thick-necked dog passes by.
He leaps up,
a scramble of fat paws,
snaps his jaws onto my right hand.
I hear the bones snap.

I float in a yellow raft,
trail my right hand in water;
clumps of green moss
darkly drift on glass.
An alligator
shatters the surface.
Massive head,
grinning smile,
pointed teeth.
My arm travels down its white throat.

Dr. Kim nods when I tell him.
"Such dreams are common for amputees."

"Why?" I ask.

"I guess the brain is working overtime.
Trying to come up with an explanation for
why your arm hurts so much."

Really, brain, you get a zero for creativity.
Why invent a dog
or an alligator
when you've been with a shark?

Team Play

Doctor
Occupational therapist
Rehab coordinator
Psychologist
Physical therapist
Amputee

We are all one big team,
they tell me. Sport shirts with collars,
big silver wristwatches.
Clipboards in hand.
One big team working
to put Jane together again.

But I'm the dead weight,
fumbling the sheets on the bed I'm supposed to make,
as across the room, someone missing
both his forearms
makes his bed with only a small wrinkle.
I am embarrassed to try the mixing bowl,
pretend to wash dishes,
practice writing, or
go through my range-of-motion moves.

Everyone is patient,
too patient,

nodding while I wait for them
to scream, "Try again, you big baby."

Instead they say,
"The goal
is not to work hard.
The goal
is to work every day."

They should dump me.
Alone, the team's energy
would send them sailing into rays of sunshine,
a scene of happy green,
a yellow finish line
and picnics where somebody's mom
passes out blue ribbons.

They give their best.
They should give it to someone better.

If Only

If only this had not happened.

Why did I go swimming right then?

If only the beach had been closed.

Why don't they have better ways of tracking sharks?
    They should protect people.

If only the amputation had been below the elbow.

Things would be easier.

It's Not Art

Mom has her laptop today.
"I bought some software I thought you'd like.
You paint with it.
The computer can do all different textures.
There's even one that looks like oil paint."

I let her talk until she sighs.
"Jane, you are so stubborn."

A mouse and a monitor are not art.
We've been over this before.
Art is meant to travel from your heart
to your head
and out through your fingers
onto *paper,* or clay, or a chapel ceiling.
Not into a mouse
into wires
into a box.

"Just *look* at it,"
she says, and
because she is Mom
and has spent the last four weeks
living in that blue chair,
I let her set it up.
When she opens the case,
I get a whiff of air freshener,

lemon oil,
the smell of home.
My heart aches.

"Okay, here it is. This over here is your brush size—
no, wait. That's your texture.
I'm not sure what this is—"

"Mom, just let me do it."
I clasp the mouse.
Mom's eyes are like stiff fingers
pressing down on my shoulders.
"Mom—"

She reaches for her purse.
"Want anything from the cafeteria?
I'll be back soon."

In the silence, I sit there,
clicking, clicking.
Someone pages Dr. Chambers.
A telephone jingles across the hall.
My lines are jerky.
I keep clicking before I mean to.
Ten minutes pass before
there emerges
a lifeless giraffe,
pasted onto a blotchy background
that looks like real oil paint.

The pen

is lying on top of my lunch menu.
It's Mom's expensive pen, the pen
with black ink
that flows like silk.
No paper.
Just a gum wrapper at the bottom of my bedside table
     trash bag.
So small —
my left hand so clumsy.

One stroke almost eats up the whole wrapper,
but I try again
and make a circle —
shaky,
feathery,
crooked —
but it is a circle.
Two eyes,
they don't land where I want them,
but they are looking back at me.
Two ears,
much rounder than planned;
a neck
that becomes skinnier and skinnier
until it meets in a point;
some spots
that are ragged;

a muzzle
that is a watermelon,
but it is a muzzle
and those are spots
and it *is* a giraffe.

It is not the giraffe
I pictured,
But it has eyes
that wait
in its lopsided head.

I hear Mom chatting with a nurse.
The wrapper, crumpled,
tucked under my pillow,
Mom exclaiming over the
sickly spotted creature on the screen.
"I TOLD you it was worth a try."
She sips her coffee.
"Oh, don't look at me like that.
Give this a chance, okay?
Jane, you are so stubborn."

I want her to leave again.
I want to be alone with Raffie,
my gum wrapper pal.
I want that pen
back in my hand.
I'll try a horse this time,

but I never could draw
with anyone watching me.

Mom is so disappointed,
I'm tempted to show her my drawing.
But I can't stomach
any phone calls to relatives,
whispers,
"Jane drew a picture today with her left hand.
Yes, I think she may try to get back into it.
Isn't it great?
So therapeutic.
But of course, her plans to become
a *professional* artist
are over."

I won't say a word.
But before Mom leaves,
I'll ask
for another piece of gum.

Hot

I remember
the sand burned my feet as I walked
toward the gray water.
I passed a lady;
a heavy lady,
carrying a thin tray
piled with three hot dogs
and three drinks.
Two little kids
pulled at her shorts.
One was crying.
A cup toppled from the tray,
splattered into the sand at my feet.
I paused, then I kept going
without looking at her face,
even as I heard her sigh,
even as the one kid
cried louder.
I felt embarrassed for her,
I'm not sure why.
I stepped into the icy water
and spread my arms wide.

The Gang

Finally, Angie, Trina, and Elizabeth
visit. Elizabeth gives me a big hug.
She cries a little. "God, I was so scared.
I thought you might die."
"We all thought that," Trina says,
hugging me too, smelling of roses
from the bouquet by her side. She adds,
"I think you're amazing.
I think you are, like, the strongest person I know."
She turns to place her flowers near the others.
"Have enough flowers, Jane? Geez, who are these
     from?"
"A secret admirer?" Angie asks.

Is she serious?
"They're from people who, you know,
saw the video and wanted to . . ."
"You are kidding," Angie says.
"No."
"Oh my God. That is so weird."
"Yeah. Maybe when you guys leave,
you could take them with you."

Trina is biting her lip.
"We wanted to come see you yesterday,
but *Angie* was busy."

Angie blushes. "I had two soccer games yesterday.
I am the referee—what am I supposed to do?"
"Well, here we are today, anyway," Elizabeth says.
"But Rachel couldn't make it."

"Yeah, she called me," I say, and
I wonder why Elizabeth and Trina
didn't come alone yesterday.
"We ran into Chris and Mason and all those guys
at the Plaza," Trina says.
"They wanted to know how you are."

"I had this great idea," Angie says.
"I want to throw you a party when you get out."
"Very funny."
"What? I'm serious."
"Angie, look at me.
Do you really think I want to have a party?"
Even I am surprised by the way
my voice just kind of
rose up and spilled out so loud. I'm not
supposed to say these things.
I'm the glue, the one that always
holds the group together, smoothing
over bumps and offenses.
"I mean, I appreciate it, but . . ."

"That's okay, I wasn't really thinking,"
Angie says.
"I'm sorry."

God, can't they see the truth?
Forget boys. Forget anything.
Dates? Kisses?
Dancing, my arm and a half around some guy?
It's over before it's even begun.

After an awkward pause,
Trina changes the subject to Troy, her latest crush.
We all try very hard to pretend
we are the same group as before,
and that nothing has changed.

A Letter from Lynn in Louisiana

Dear Jane,

I saw your story on the news. Honey, my heart goes out to you. It is unbelievable that something so horrible could happen to someone so young. Do you remember what happened? It must have been awful. I am amazed that they show that video on the news as often as they do. Even with the really bad parts blurred out, it sure seems like an invasion of your privacy to do so.

Well, Jane, I just want you to know that my whole church is praying for you to recover and overcome this terrible time in your life. We have you in our prayer chain and pray for you at every service, too. We love you and think of you every day. I am sure God will deliver you from this pain and He will carry you down the path of healing. Sometimes it is not easy to understand why God allows us to suffer, but always there is an answer if you just wait and listen with your heart. Pray to God, Jane, and pray to Jesus and I can promise you that they will send comfort.

God works in mysterious ways, but always He is loving to those who believe.

Love to you and your family.

Your sister in Christ,

Lynn

Smaller Picture

And then . . . some days are gray days,
vast, unbearable
canyon days, when I can't take
the frantic buzzing in my arm anymore.
"My life is going to be one long hurt,"
I tell Mel. Sick as it is, I say it:
"Sometimes I wish I died."

"Time to think about the *smaller* picture,"
Mel says. "Like getting through one day.
Not your whole life, not forever,
one day.
Sometimes we can only look at one hour,
or one minute."

Tears crawl into my eyes.
Emptiness makes my throat ache.

"On those bad days, Jane,
hold on. Get through one minute.
Then tell yourself,
I made it through that minute,
I can make it through another."

So I do as he says,
and get through
one   more   day.

Self

Some nights,
in between the clatter of medical carts
that rumble by,
and the endless vacuuming
outside my door,

I dream of my old self.
Two arms,
two hands,
drawing. Always drawing.
The lines thick
and black.
The animals I used to sketch,
their eyes, watching.

During the steamy noon hour
while Mom goes for lunch,
I take the pen and notepad
and scratch away.
Wobbly foxes,
trees; levitating,
one-dimensional clouds.

I trash everything
before Mom returns.

I will continue in
this vein until those trees
take root, and clouds become cotton.
I will surprise everyone,
showing my work only
when I am good again.
Good.

Again.

Invisible

Nurse: "You're so brave, Jane."
Hospital volunteer: "You are a hero."
Physical therapist: "You're a real survivor, know that?"

When people talk like that,
I could get up and slip away
and they'd still stand there,
talking to the cartoon cloud
they've drawn over my body.

Just once,
I'd like someone to say,
"Jane, you are a mess."

Justin

There's a new kid in the physical therapy gym today.
His name is Justin.
Justin is around eight or nine or ten maybe.
He's lost his leg below the knee
in some kind of car accident.
His face is all cut up, too.
Justin rolls over in his wheelchair.
"What happened to your arm?" he asks.

"A shark attacked me."

Justin stares. "He ATE your arm?"
I feel sorry for him; so skinny and messed up.
But I don't need some kid bugging me.
I move away but Justin follows,
silent and smooth in his wheelchair.
He asks,
"Have you seen the new Superman movie?"
I haven't.
Justin goes into the whole long, long story,
complete with explosion sound effects.
I wait to see what this has to do with me or my arm
or the attack.
Nothing.
Justin just wants to talk about Superman.

I like Justin.

Try to Acknowledge

Mom watches me return
from a loop around the hall
with Lindsey.
"Moving any better today?"
she asks, all cheer.

I slide into bed
one piece at a time.
"Not really."

Mom sighs loudly.
"It *seems* like you are moving
better. Sometimes I think
you don't look for encouragement,
Jane. Try to acknowledge
your progress. You *are* making progress."

Lindsey chimes in.
"You sure are, Jane.
You are doing just great."
Then Lindsey surprises us
by putting a hand on Mom's shoulder.
"And you are too, Katherine.
Really, really great."

Mom blinks back tears,
but pretends not to.

Wiping her eyes, she pats Lindsey
on the back,
reaches down for her newspaper,
sits in the chair.
"We're *all* doing great," she says,
sniffing loudly. "Which is good.
I have to get back to work
sometime."

"Sorry if I'm keeping you,"
I hear myself say, harsh and ugly.
"You could go in if you want. I'll be fine."

Mom looks up, wipes her nose quickly.
"I didn't mean that, of course.
I just meant . . .
well, you know."
I don't.
But I don't ask her to explain.

Finally, she murmurs,
"I'm going downstairs for some coffee."

When she's gone,
I can finally let these stupid tears
come out.

Private Affair

Mom sinks into the blue
vinyl chair by the bed.
"I'm going to have a few sessions
with Mel."

I stare at her
over my pudding cup.
"Why?"

She smooths the knees
of her pants,
smoothing and smoothing
with slow, firm movements.
"Well. He thinks, as family,
Michael and I should
talk about what happened.
Talk about how we're feeling.
But Michael won't go.
So it will be just me."

"Oh."
I put the cup aside.
Outside the window,
the sun shines brightly,
the sky is clean. Tops
of palm trees sway slightly
in a breeze.

"It will probably only be
a couple of times," Mom adds.

We don't look at each other.

What is this? She's not stealing
a guy I like, a best friend, or anything like that.
But I'm upset.
Maybe because my mother
needs therapy
to deal with this thing,
this thing that is me
that has disrupted
not just my life
but hers, too.
That's what hurts.

That I've caused her this.
And that she and Mel will
discuss
behind that closed door
what Mom is feeling.

What *is* she feeling?
I wish
I could be a fly on the wall
when she begins.

Pinned Up

Justin drew me a picture.
Blobby men with stick legs
and a sausage roll with long ears.
"That's my parents and my dog, Spot."
"You have a dog named *Spot?*" I ask.
He nods. "I miss her."

I ask Michael to tape the drawing to the wall.
"You're a good artist, Justin," he says.
"Jane's an artist, too."
Justin turns those blue eyes on me.
"Will you draw me a—"
"No."
"Why not?"
"I lost my hand, Justin. I can't draw anymore."

He points to my left hand.
"But you could use that one."

"I can't, okay, Justin? It's not my good hand."
Justin looks down. "*Both* my legs were good.
But now I only have one, so it's the good one.
Isn't it that way with your arm?"

He doesn't get it. No one gets it.
I wish they would all leave me
alone.

A Message

Mom always waits for me
outside of Mel's office.
She walks me back up
to my room.
Always smiles at Mel,
says, "Thank you."
She waits until we're in the elevator
to look at my face,
searching for red eyes.
Her hand warms my shoulder,
hugging with her fingers.

One day, after Mom meets me,
starts to turn us away,
I catch Mel's look.
In that instant
he sends me a silent message.
"You need each other."

We step into the elevator. The flickering light
makes our skin appear blue.
I feel Mom's fingers on my shoulder,
soft, steady.
I reach up and touch her hand.

Both of us are surprised.

Why?

In the gym today
Justin fell down.
His new leg shifted sideways
when he got out of a chair.
He fell down
and he cried.
Justin has never cried in therapy before.
I hate life.

Don't even tell me
God has a reason
for making Justin suffer.
Or me, either. He wouldn't.
Would he?

I wish I could fix things for him,
for me. For everyone.
I wish I knew
why some people live

and some people die
and some people

get stuck

in the middle.

Visitors

Grandma and Grandpa are leaving today.
Aunt Karen and Uncle Ben arrive in time to say hello,
trade hugs and thumps on the back,
high voices, the smell of hairspray from Gram,
pillowy cheeks and lined faces
touched to mine; careful kisses.
As Mom prepares to go home,
everyone shuffles out into the hall together.
Whispering ensues—
I know they're talking about me.

That's what they're here for, I guess.
To assure themselves *I'm* still here.
I want them to sit by my bed
and tell me the news from Kansas,
but I want them to leave, too.

I want
to experience stillness.

A Letter from Kristen,
Whitefish Bay, Wisconsin

Dear Jane,

I read about your story in the newspaper. My heart goes out to you. You are so young, and, judging by the picture in the paper, so beautiful. I have been in your place, Jane, and I am writing because if you're anything like me you could use an encouraging word right now.

My left leg was amputated above the knee ten years ago, after an accident at work in which I nearly died. At first I shut myself off from the rest of the world, even the people I loved. But then I joined a support group for amputees and let me tell you, it was the best thing in the world for me. It helps to see you're not the only one going through all the adjustments that come with amputation.

I went back to work eighteen months after the accident. Not long afterward, I got engaged to my boyfriend, William, who I met through the support group. He lost both legs in a car crash. William and I married seven years ago and I've never been happier. Both of us love to be outdoors and do all kinds of sports. We swim, sail, kayak, and ski. I also take yoga and find it highly relaxing.

I'm enclosing a picture of us—I hope you don't mind. Please feel free to write or call when you are well enough, if you ever want advice or just to talk. I'd love to be friends.

Best wishes,
Kristen Miller-Capshaw

Wednesday

Jane, I'm going to go home for a while. Aunt Karen is going to stay with you.

Okay, Mom.

Hi, honey. Do you need anything? Some more water?

No, thanks, Aunt Karen. I'm fine.

Ben and I are staying in your room back home. I hope you don't mind, but I was looking through your bookshelves last night.

I don't mind.

I didn't know you had so many cookbooks. I didn't know vegetarians had so many great recipes. Your mom said you like to cook. That you do most of the cooking during the week.

Yeah, well, I guess I won't be doing that anymore.

You'll learn how. You don't need two hands to cook.

Mmm.

You sure have some nice art books, too. Would you like me to bring some in for you to read?

Uh, no. That's okay.

I don't mind.

I don't want to read art books right now.

Well, I brought all your Harry Potter books. See? I'll put them over here. Your mom says you always read these when you're down.

How would she . . .

What, honey?

Nothing. Thanks, but I don't feel like reading.

Oh. Well, I'll just put them over here. By the roses, see? On top of these cards. Goodness.

What?

So many cards.

Uncle Ben?

Hey there, how was that shower?

Where's Mom?

She had to go to work, hun. I'm going to sit with you this morning, then Karen will be over this afternoon. Okay?

Sure.

Uh, do you need help with that gown, that, uh . . .

If you could just call the nurse, she'll tie it for me.

Right.

(Later)

You know, Jane, I have a friend who was struck by lightning. Burned all the skin on the left side of his body. He lost his hearing and was disfigured for life.

Really.

Yep. But you know, he never lost his faith in God? Never questioned why that happened to him and not someone else. Can you imagine?

No.

(Long pause.)

I've been asking God about this, Jane. And I think as bad as it is, we have to remember how close you came to death. I don't know why this happened, but I believe in my heart that God saved your life that day.

(Pause.)

You think I'm full of baloney, don't you?

No! I just . . . I don't know. It's hard to feel grateful.

I understand.

(Pause.)

Oh, Lord, I didn't mean to make you cry, Janie.

I'm sorry. It's just that my arm hurts today. It hurts so much.

Should I get the nurse? Will they give you something?

They already did. I have to wait now until my next shot.

Come here. Oh, honey, come here and let me hold you. It's okay. You cry on me as much as you want, all right? Just cry on your uncle Ben.

I feel so stupid.

Why? Jane, don't even say that. If I were in your shoes, I'd be crying, too. Don't you know how brave you've been? You have a lot to cry about, and don't ever apologize for it. It's part of healing. The tears wash away the pain.

I remember you telling me that when I was little. That time I fell down off my bike and broke my finger.

Oh, yes, I remember that. Such a tough little thing you were. Just like your mother.

Really?

Oh, yes. She was so stubborn when she was your age. Like you are now. But you know something? Her stubbornness has done her good. I thought she'd die of grief when your father passed away, but she just dug in her heels and refused to give up. Went back to school, finished her degree, got a good paying job to support you and your brother.

Yeah . . .

And your stubbornness is going to pay off for you, too.
Something like this, losing your arm, honey, that's
enough to make some people lie down and die. But not
you. That's not going to happen to you.

I'm never going to draw again, Uncle Ben. Not well,
anyway.

(Pause.) You will, too. When you're ready, you will. You
have a gift too special to give up on.

It won't be the same.

I know.

Nothing is ever going to be the same.

It's all right. (Pause.) Is there a tissue box around here
somewhere?

Here, you can have mine.

You've got me going, too.

Two Books

One day Mel hands me a book.
"A journal," he says. "It'll help."
I thank him,
wondering how long it would take me
to scratch out one page.
What would I write about, anyway?
"I won't read it," Mel adds.
"But bring it next time.
Just so I can make sure
you've written something.
Anything.
This is not a suggestion, Jane.
It's a prescription."

"Oh."
So that's the way it is.
In that case, I don't want this book.
I don't need this. Besides—
this book is too snooty.
It has a spiral spine,
to lay open without help,
but still,
that richly textured leather cover,
the highbrow papers that shriek expensive,
daring you to misspell or cross out.
Heaven forbid—an inkblot.
"Thanks, Mel, but I don't want to waste this nice—"

Mel reaches deep into a desk drawer,
whips out a cheap purple notebook.
"There you are, Miss Artistic Temperament.
Whichever suits your mood.
See you Tuesday."

I walk out,
both books in the crook of my arm.
I feel like I have been handed the keys
to a cage of lions.

Thoughts on a Tuesday Morning

I don't want the night nurse
to rewrap my "residual limb,"
because she's not gentle and doesn't care,
and once she asked me if I remembered seeing a fin.

I don't want this burning in my arm
to wake me from a dream of gliding through water
without fear.

I want to clap my hands.
I want to tie my shoes.

Today Justin asked me if I hated everybody.
"You look like you do," he said.
"You would, too, if your story was all over the news," I told him.
"Those people who write to me. They tell me they love me.
They don't even know me."

Justin thought for a moment.
His eyes are so blue.
He said, "You don't have to love everybody.
But you have to love your family. We're nice people."
Justin includes himself in my family,
not even thinking about it.

I think
I love Justin.

Go Fish

I used to whine, I remember with shame.
My world is too small, this town is too boring,
California is disgusting. I wanted to expand,
probe my world,
backpack through Europe.
Now,
I deal cards to Justin and me,
while his mom steps out for lunch.
"Do you have any kings?" Justin asks,
and it's "Go fish" for him.

The simple pleasure he gets from this silly game,
it keeps his mind off the pain, I can see it,
and when he asks if I want to play again,
I say yes, of course.
"Shuffle," he commands.
I sigh. "Can't. Remember?
You need two hands to shuffle."
Justin laughs. "Oops. Sorry."

I watch him shuffle, furrowing his brows in concentration,
and I could sit in cramped hospital room #323,
never leaving Justin's side.
I let him win, I see him smile,
and my world
is big
enough.

Warm Hands

The night nurse, Carole, doesn't smile, rarely speaks.
Her hands are warm, but
she pushes that thermometer into my ear too hard,
never checks my water pitcher.
She watches, impassively, while I shuffle to the bathroom.

My day nurse, Lindsey,
shows me pictures of her son,
brings me a share of his homemade cookies.
Her hands are cold, but steady.
We loop these halls like a geriatric hamster
on a wheel.
She knows when to talk
or when to get silent,
as I ride a tide of pain until it passes.

Palm to cheek.
My hand
is cold.
I could do it,
I could help like Lindsey,
knowing what I know now.

The difference between two warm hands
and someone who cares
is all the difference
in the world.

Looking at Mel

He helps me feel better.
He helps me make sense
of the days to come.

I could do that.
For someone else.
I know what it means
to know someone
listens.

Sketching
weak-kneed horses,
I think about

nursing. Therapy. Rehab.
Careers I
never thought of before.
Now, returning the pen
beside the phone,
I think about it

some more.

Shuffled

Today he wheels himself to my room
to say
good-bye.
"I'll call you," he says.
His skinny arms quick around my neck.
How can I stay in this place without Justin?

"Will you draw me a picture?" I ask.
"I will, if you'll draw one for me," he says.

"Mmm. You say hi to Spot for me, okay?"

Justin slips something into my hand.
"You keep these."
It is the deck of cards
we've nearly worn out together.

"You can shuffle them by laying them on the bed
and mixing them around," he says.

There is an emptiness
filling my throat, and I can
hardly speak.
"Thanks."

Justin's mother places a slim hand
on my shoulder. Her gold wedding band

glints under the fluorescent light.
"Thank *you,* Jane.
You've been such a friend to him.
I can't imagine what we'd have done without you."

I watch from the window
as far below, Justin and his mom wait as
Justin's dad rolls up in their new van.
Small Justin rising from his big wheelchair,
leans on his mother's arm,
turns, looks up at my window, squinting,
and waves.

I wave back, and I watch that van
take Justin away,
the deck of cards, warm,
still stacked
in my palm.

July 25

Mel fidgets; I sit like a stone.
Our last session.
I have so much to say.
Why didn't I say it?
Where did the hours go?

"Good-byes are the hardest
part of the job, Jane. How are you
feeling about going home?"

A shrug. I try not to cry.

"Tell me, Jane. Nervous?"

"Wouldn't you be?"

That gets him to smile. Then
I can smile, too. When we hug,
I realize again that Mel is an old man.
His shoulders are as frail as Justin's.
He has just seemed strong.

Probably

He's probably glad to see you go.

Shut up. Mel likes me.

Come on. You're a big whiner. He's in there right now, saying "Thank God she's gone."

Stop it. Why do I do this to myself?

Probably because you're too weak to handle this.

I am not. Stop.

You're weak.

No.

Weak.

Good-Byes Are Fattening

"Let's hear it for Jane!"
Shrieks of joy,
a smattering of clapping,
beaming faces, shining eyes,
gathered around my bed.
The nurses' smiles send the temperature in this room
soaring.

"We have something for you," Lindsey says,
stepping around Dr. Kim.
She and Mel open a large white box between them,
revealing a cake.
Pink frosted roses and yellow writing:
Good-bye, Jane. We'll miss you.

All these nurses,
and volunteers and doctors,
Mom and Michael and Rachel,
all gathered around.
Lindsey is crying,
the lady who brings my flowers blows her nose,
Michael passes out plates, intent on cake.

Everyone eats and talks quickly,
since they all have somewhere to be;
a man steps forward,

leans in to pat my shoulder.
I see by his uniform, he's a paramedic.

"I'm one of the ones who brought you in,"
he says. His tag reads MARTY.
His crinkled face makes me guess he's fifty or so,
the age my dad would be, maybe.
"I've been wanting to come visit you," Marty says,
"but I didn't want to bug you. I'm so glad you're okay.
When we brought you in, I didn't know if . . .
well. I didn't know.
I have a girl at home your age."

His words sort of
pour over me
and go away somewhere.
I'm not ready to think about what Marty saw
the day he lifted me off the sand.
But quick as you please,
I've swept up his job, too.
A paramedic? I wonder if I can do that
with one arm.
I bet I'd be good, if it *is* possible.
Helping. Being the first one there.
Saving a life,
talking to someone scared.

"Thank you," I tell Marty, and he departs,
Mel pressing a plate of cake
into Marty's large hands.
Michael grins at me,
plops a dab of pink frosting
on my nose. "Hey, cupcake,"
he says. Not funny. But
for some stupid reason,
we both burst out laughing.
It feels rusty,
but it feels great.

Leaving

I'm going home.
My own bed.
My dog.
My stuff.
But I'm standing here staring at my hospital bed
as if it's a lifeboat.
This bed
where I lay in a coma
for ten days,
where my family
ate, slept, and lived.
It's *my* bed.

These halls
where I walked in my wrinkled gown,
trailing the I.V. stand,
a stiff, leaning creeper,
I know these halls.

This bedside table
where I ate a million cold turkey dinners
with congealed potatoes,
breakfasts of cold oatmeal,
warm orange juice
that burned my throat;
it wasn't bad.
Not bad at all.

That window.
That's the problem.
Justin and I would sit there at night
after our families had gone home.
We'd make up stories
about the people we saw down in the parking lot.
"That man with the flowers is coming to see his new baby,"
Justin would say.
My turn.
"That woman, the one crying,
she just got some bad news about her husband."
I put a negative spin on everything.
But at Justin's look, I tried to be more optimistic.
"That family over there, the ones getting back into their van,
they just found out their Grandma is all better
and they're running home to bake her a cake."
Justin sighed on that one.
Guess I overdid it.

The problem is
life outside the window
is life *outside*.
Not here.
People out there
are out *there*.
Too many.

The eyes of the doctors
are familiar.
The kind of seeing I can almost live with.
It's their job, taking care of people like me.
I was welcome here.
I fit in.
Out there,
I won't.

T · W · O

Cold

I remember the water was so cold.
Goose bumps rose up on my arms.
A wave slapped me and I tasted salt.
I stood there, up to my chest,
moving my arms like I was treading water.
I looked back.
Mom waved.
I turned away without waving back,
And moved farther from shore.

Calm, 84 Percent

This is what I know
about shark attacks.

You are more likely
to die in a car crash
driving to the beach
than to be attacked once
you are there,
swimming.

Other facts:
84 percent, give or take,
happen in calm waters.

Shiny jewelry,
erratic movements,
having your period,
all are contributing factors.

Then again,

sometimes you're just
in the wrong place
at the wrong time.

Real World

Here it is.
This is where the shit hits the fan.
The Sahara desert,
and me without my survival kit.

Home.
I missed it.
But nothing
is familiar.
When did everything get so bright?
So loud,
so cluttered?
Why do I have so much stuff?

The smell of baby powder deodorant
is from another lifetime.
My dog, Mabel, white and wiggly,
barking with happiness,
she's like a clip from an old family movie.
My room, a frozen photograph—

my bed,
pillows piled high on the chair.
Robinson Crusoe on the nightstand—
I forgot I was reading that.
Makeup on the white dresser,
books on the shelves,

a rainbow of pencils on the drafting table.
It's all exactly as I left it,
but it's different.

I'm the one who's different.
Obviously.
My stomach is so tight
at the sight
of sweaters hanging in the closet,
pairs of slim sleeves
dangling
down.

The Kitchen

The couch
welcomes my body.
The rug,
furry on my feet.
The hallway
with my footsteps worn into it—
my bathroom!
Clean, bright, *private*.
I am as happy to see my bathroom
as I am to feel my own soft bed.

But the kitchen stops me.

I see myself in this room,
shorts over my pink bikini,
thumping cans of soda,
dumping trays of ice,
tossing bagged sandwiches
into our red cooler,
the one we took that day.

Always hurrying.
That was me.
If I'd only slowed down,
ten minutes more
might have been
enough.

Oil in the Machinery

By the silverware drawer,
Mom and I bump.
Forks clatter to the floor.
Stepping
into the hallway,
Michael and I crash shoulders.
In the living room,
popcorn spilled on the floor.
I bend to pick it up,
Mom reaches to help,
Mabel dives for a taste,
all three of us smack heads.

"Sorry," and "Excuse me,"
and
"Here, let me do it,"
cover up pressed lips and
big sighs.

Funny.
I've come home
one arm lighter;
one arm smaller.

So why do I take up more space than before?

The Web

Methodic pecking of the keys
reminds me how they used to clatter
when I could type.
But I surf, page after page
popping up under
"amputee."
Many sites are perky,
imparting words for thought.
*People with dis*ABILITIES,
for example,
or the Feminine Amputee Site:
It takes a "special woman"
to overcome the pitfalls of amputation.
Why the quotes?

Here's a favorite:
A rose without a petal
is still a rose.

Please.

Will I ever
feel called to respond
to post #316:
"Does anyone have any tips
for buttoning their pants?"

Okay, I read that one.

Motivational speakers.
Forums.
Chat rooms.

And overwhelmingly:
Most of the time, we become
a better person than we were.

I was *fine*
with who I was.

I will never
become one of these heroic
icons, spreading hope
from the other side,
one hand waving.

Can't

"Come with me
to the grocery store,"
Mom says.
"It's a nice day.
We can stop for ice cream
or something.
Lunch out?"

"No, thanks."

"Please, honey?"

Over my book,
I watch Mom put on
a winning smile.
I see what she's doing.
Trying to balance hope
with casualness,
trying not to push.

But the thought of stepping out
there like this—

I listen to her car drive away.
I return to my book.
But the words
don't make sense.

Pharmacy

Food was my friend.
"You are always eating,"
Rachel would say.
Mom would tell her friends,
"It's not Michael that eats the most around here,
it's my dainty little daughter."

Food is the best medicine.
That's Grandma's favorite saying.
Mine, too.
Spaghetti,
the Band-Aid for scraped feelings.
Cookies,
the aspirin for all headaches.
Pizza,
a snake-oil salve for You-Name-It.
Mashed potatoes,
the antibiotics of the Food Pharmacy.

Now,
Mom places a plate before me,
a snow-white pile of mashed potatoes,
steamy hot.
"You need to get your strength back,"
she says.
"Eat."

The food slides down warm and easy,
but leaves me gagging.
I can't take more than three bites.

Will *anything* ever be normal again?
I can't even eat.

Later, Michael brings me a stack
of magazines.
"These have good jokes in them."

"You know I don't like dirty jokes."
"Unbutton, okay? Read one."
"Why?"
Michael folds his arms. "Grandma is wrong.
Food isn't the best medicine.
Laughter is."

He walks out.
I stay up late, reading by the bedside lamp
while Mabel snores by my feet.

Three times, I chuckle.
And a warmth,
smooth and easy, like mashed potatoes,
flickers somewhere
in my heart.

Wonder

If you had helped that lady. The one with the tray of hot dogs. But oh, no. You couldn't be bothered.

I know I should have. But I was . . .

She was fat. You were embarrassed for her because she was fat.

I was not!

If she saw you today, she'd be the one embarrassed. For you. Ironic, isn't it?

Stop this. Why am I doing this?

Because you know this whole thing is your own selfish fault, and no one else does. If they only knew, what would they say?

They would say it wasn't my fault. They'd say . . .

They'd say, if you had taken the time to help, it would have been enough. It would have delayed you. And it would have never happened to you.

Maybe. Maybe not. Who knows. I'll never know.

But you'll always wonder.

I'll wonder a lot of things.

It would have been different.

I don't know that.

Different.

I don't know . . .

You do.

Monday Morning

Hello?

Jane? It's Angie.

Hi.

Whatcha doing?

I'm trying to eat this thing my mom made. I think it's an omelet.

Oh.

She's not a great cook.

Yeah, you were the cook, weren't you? Your poor mom.

Huh?

She has to do everything now. I guess you can't really vacuum or fold laundry or any of that stuff anymore?

Well, no.

I'm almost jealous.

Angie—

IknowIknowIknow. I'm kidding. Really. Sorry, that was a sick joke. You know I'm kidding, right?

I certainly *hope* so.

I was calling to see if you wanted to come with me to the mall today. Elizabeth is going and Rachel said she'd see. Trina can't.

Why not?

Hmm? I don't know, she's going out with her family somewhere. Want to?

I don't think so.

We're supposed to meet some guys there.

Who?

Well, we don't know for sure yet, but Alex Cussaks and Scotty Anderson are supposed to be there. I saw them last night at the movies and we talked about hooking up. They said they might come with some other guys, maybe Taylor Pocheck or Ty Zacks. So, how about it? Could be fun!

No, I don't want to.

Are you worried about—you know. People being weird about your arm?

Well, of course.

Jane, they're going to see you when school starts. Why not get it out of the way?

I'm not ready. And I'm kind of tired.

Come on. Please?

No, thanks. Really.

Really?

Really.

Can't change your mind?

No.

Okay . . . well, we should get together sometime, though. Us.

Yeah, that would be great.

Mom

Mom bends down to tie my shoes.
The tag of her shirt is sticking up
out of her collar along her neck.
I tuck it back in.

"Thanks," she says, and smiles briefly.
This catches me off guard.
She doesn't smile much anymore.
"You're welcome," I say,
and I force a little smile in return.

She looks surprised.

I wonder
if she's thinking
the same exact thing
about me.

Moat, Overlooking

I am on the floor,
straddled,
my portfolio spread before me.

I was pretty good.
But the subject matter . . .

Rabbit, Hopping.
Blue mountains, sagebrush,
a hawk, soaring.
Bowls of tulips,
in pastel, pencil,
crayon, and acrylic.
A house,
smoke rising from the chimney.

These pictures
are from someone else's world,
someone else's memories,
not mine.

What, then, is now?
If I can't return to
Horse, Grazing,
am I doomed to be a
van Gogh imitation?
Tortured, wrecked, surviving

pain through the art of my darkest attic,
creations spun from the haunted memories
of the Shark Girl
trying to accommodate with her left hand?
Will the subject matter
be endless grays and white-capped
waves, gaunt faces, thin children,
rain?

I have no legs
to cross the bridge
toward Sunflower, Blooming,
and return home.

Author

I try to fill Mel's journal.
It will help, he said.
Writing a bit each day,
sparsely. The words don't
come easily. Never have. I'm not
much of a storyteller. But . . .

I could tell my story.
The Shark Girl's story.
And out of a shark's bite
could arise a fresh, raw
writer, poignant, powerful,
with a story that would win a Pulitzer.
I could.

Then I remember.
I don't like to write,
and I don't want to *learn*
to like to write.
Oh,
and my life is private.

So back to my entry.

Today
I got dressed by myself.

Waiting

Mom slides both hands
into her pockets.
"Ready for some lunch?
No, it's okay, I'll fix it for you.

Just tell me what you want."

She takes my order
and leaves, light in step.
It used to be my job,
a job I loved—
making my own lunch,
preparing our dinners weeknights,
whipping up snacks
for our weekend munchies.

But,
come to think of it,
I haven't fixed a single meal
since I came back home.

Mom's done them all.

August 15

Tonight, over pizza,
Michael gives us the silent treatment.
Mom shrugs it off before taking Mabel for a walk.
I hang around the kitchen a bit, watching Michael clean up.
I say, "Want me to help with that?"
He whirls, eyebrows high.
"Really? You mean it? Gosh, I'm so *honored*."

"What is your problem?" I ask.
Michael slams the pizza box shut.
"I'm tired of doing everything around here.
Just because you make Mom wait on you,
doesn't mean *I* will."

While Michael takes out the trash
and wipes off the table,
I empty the plates, load the dishwasher,
and put away the extra salad.
My throat hurts and I cannot look at my brother.
When we're done, Michael
tosses the towel
into the sink.

Who the hell does he think he is?
What an ass. A candidate for Mr. Insensitivity.
For the first time since June,
I hate him.

Tired All the Time

The shakes,
the cold night sweats,
soaking
hot sheets
that tangle around my legs,
thinking,
the memory obliterated, but
imagining the shape
of a fish,
a *fish,*
sliding through the water,
a silent gray missile,
triangular teeth in gaping mouth,
clamping down —
Did it really happen?

The movie in my head
loops
while the moon
floats
from one end of the window
to the other,
then fades

away.

In the Morning

I lie on the couch,
watching TV.
Mom zips the vacuum around the room,
Michael starts to step outside
and gets snatched back.
"I asked you to do the dusting
and empty the dishwasher," Mom says.
Michael slams the door,
stomps into the kitchen,
and mercilessly crashes the dishes into the cupboard.
He leaves the house
with a black cloud around his head.
"Grump," Mom mutters,
and returns to mopping,
the squish of water
moving
farther
away.

Finally, it is quiet
enough to slide
into sleep,
safe
in the daylight.

Adrift

"There's a support group at the hospital,"
Mom says. "You could go."

I know better than to say "No,"
outright. "Maybe. Sometime."
Mom sighs and leaves me
crumbling toast across my plate.
"See you tonight, honey."

Walking Mabel down the street,
wearing a bulky sweater in the broiling
heat, so as to better hide my missing limb,
I think about the Internet sites I have found.

There's a community out there,
broken people like me, pressing on,
and maybe some of them are doing just fine;
many are now better people, according to them.
But really, aren't most of them pretending?
Aren't most of us pretending
all the time,
able-bodied or not?

Before,
I drifted, separate
from the flow,

watched land masses of fellow students
shift and merge, part and dissolve,
all the while
putting forth my own small beacon
of calm, confident belonging.
All false.
I'd figure it out eventually, I thought.

Where is the truth now?
Where can I find that line to stand upon,
step into the stream of humanity,
the place that is mine?

I am reflecting on this
while Mabel investigates a bush.
When someone passes,
murmuring, "Good morning,"
and brushes their sleeve against mine,
the touch is like a magnet,
so powerful
my whole body turns
toward them,
wanting to stick.

If only I could grab hold of something,
and hold tight.

Take a Picture

Driving home from physical therapy,
Mom announces, "I have to stop
at the store for a few things."
Great.
I know Mom.
A "few things"
means she'll be half an hour.
"I'll wait in the car."

Mom protests.
"It's too hot. You'll roast.
I'd rather not leave the AC
on, honey. You know how the car is.
It will over—"
"I'll be fine," I tell her.
I won't let her win this one.
She will not make me go inside.

But of course,
ten minutes later,
the parking lot
is swimming in shimmers,
sweat crawls down my neck,
I am growing dizzy,
and I have to step out
and find Mom.

The guy at the sandwich counter
studies me like I'm an animal in the zoo.

A woman in the fruit section
stands with a cantaloupe in her hand,
the empty scale dangling beside her,
staring. At me.

Walking too quickly, I bump into a girl
rounding the corner. She drops
a bag of pretzels.
When I try to help her
she exclaims,
"It's okay, really!"

God. Get me out of here.
Finally Mom is snared by
the frozen peaches.
"What is taking you so long?"
I say.
"Sorry," Mom says. "I'm almost done."
Then,
I feel the tears welling up,
and I smash them down.
Two boys, passing, look,
and look again.

I want to shout to everyone
that my new arm will be ready soon,

that I will wear it every minute
when I get it
so no one
will have an excuse to do a double take.
But all I do, of course,
is cling to the cart like I'm five years old,
and follow Mom
as she guides us both
to the checkout.

Forever

Missing an arm is like wearing a coat,
a really big, hot, ugly coat
that I can't take off.
Ever.
It's all that people see.

Before this happened,
once in a while I would see someone.
Someone without a leg or an arm.
My stomach would flip,
I'd look away fast,
then look back,
a crawling sensation behind my belly button.
I'd wonder about them.

Now I'm one of those people
and people wonder about me.
I get that crawling sensation
just thinking about it.

Fat

Angie and Trina
come to visit. They look so pretty.
Skinny Angie's makeup is perfect,
Trina wears new black sandals.
She scoops up wiggly Mabel,
kissing Mabel's curly white-haired head.
"I missed this dog."

Mom offers us brownies
she has made,
but they are so dry
we smile and disappear upstairs to my room.

"You guys, I am *so* fat,"
Angie moans,
sprawling across my bed.
"I don't know what's wrong with me.
I've been eating like a pig."
She pulls at the waistband
of her jeans.
"See? I can barely zip."

"Yeah, you're taking up the whole room,
you must be a size *two* by now,"
Trina says, rolling her eyes.
She catches sight of my drawing table.

She fingers the pens.
"Jane, have you tried drawing again yet?"
I hear myself lie.
"No."

Angie and Trina exchange looks.
"You will, though, right?"
Trina asks.
Angie sits up. "You should."
I shrug. "Yeah, I will.
Sometime."

For a moment,
we all listen to a crow,
cawing outside.
Then we resume talking
about Angie's fat.
"You have to *make* me
watch what I eat!" she says.

And this talk is fine.

It's better
than the
bare-boned
truth.

Rice and Beans

Uncooked
red beans, black beans, white rice,
filling up a wide glass jar.
Pretty enough
to sit on a shelf just for looking.
Instead,
I stick my stump
inside the jar,
and roll it around,
feeling.
Rough and smooth.
Grainy on my flesh.
Doctor's orders.
Desensitization, in preparation for my prosthesis.
Does it get any weirder than this?

A Letter from Paul Shaylor, Age 16

To Jane Arrowood,

My name is Paul Shaylor. I am writing because my English teacher, Miss Felix, is making us do a nonfiction report. We have to interview somebody about something and write a report about it like it's a newspaper column. I saw the video on TV. The newspeople said you're home now. Will you interview with me?

You could e-mail me or call me, or maybe just fill out these questions on a separate sheet of paper.

1. *What happened when the shark attacked you?*
2. *When did you find out you had to have your arm amputated? What did the doctors say?*
3. *Are you going to get a fake arm? If so, what is that like? How much does one cost? How long will it take to learn to use it?*
4. *Do you hate sharks now? Do you think you'll ever go swimming again?*
5. *What kind of things did you like to do before you lost your arm?*
6. *Do you think you'll do most of those things again, or not?*
7. *Do you have any advice for anyone going swimming? On how to protect themselves from sharks?*

Thanks for helping me.

Sincerely,

Paul

The Hook

I'm not thankful for much these days.
But I thank heaven and lucky stars
that Dr. Kim was straight with me
about my prosthesis.
"It's not going to do the things your hand
could do.
Give it six months, then decide."

Open, close. Click,
click.
Sam, the prosthesis maker,
demonstrates the metal hook attachment.
"It's not the most attractive thing in the world,"
he says. "But it is functional. There are other options,
    too."

Mom is silent.
There's a cosmetic arm,
with "skin" that looks soft and smooth.
"Doesn't do anything,
but gives some people confidence," Sam says.
"Some patients wear it
when they're on a date,
or a job interview, or just walking around.
It depends on how you feel."

I could tell him how I feel.

This *place* feels like mannequin purgatory.
It's unbelievable
that I belong here. *Need* to be here.
I wonder what makes a person
want to make artificial limbs for a living.

"I love it," Sam replies.
"I get to meet some pretty fascinating people.
Like you. Your mom said on the phone
that you are an artist?"

Mom has the decency to blush.

"I *was,*" I tell Sam.

"You still can be, you know," Sam says. "I had a—"
I shut him up quick. I don't want to hear any more
inspirational stories. I'm sick of them.

"Do people ever have more than one prosthesis?" I ask.
Sam nods. "Yes, most have one functional
and one cosmetic."

After a discussion over insurance,
we order both.
But I'm thinking:

I can't wear that thing.
I won't.
It's an insult.

"It's not bad enough people lose arms,"
I say to Sam and Mom.
"But on top of it,
we're supposed to look like Captain Hook?"

Sam regards me seriously.
"You are a very attractive girl, Jane.
Inside and out. I can tell.
I think you'll find
the more comfortable you are with yourself,
the more people won't notice your prosthesis.
Or absence of one,
if that's how you eventually choose to go.
I think that you'll find . . ."

I let him prattle on.
He's trying to help.
But obviously, he's never been
in my shoes.
So aside from the medical part,
what
does he know?

Constant

Fixing me lunch. Fixing me snacks.
Hanging around while I talk on the phone.
Mom hovers like a fly, buzzing.
"Don't forget to—"
"Be sure and—"
"No. Not that way."
Reminding me
about *everything* I already know.
"Buckle that strap; no, *that* one . . ."
two seconds before I plan on doing it.
"Now clean that socket before you put on your
        prosthesis,
and after you take it off.
You don't want it to get an odor."
"I know!" escapes my lips.
Then
hurt eyes,
pouting,
silence.
"I'm just trying to help" hangs heavy in the air.
Sometimes her "help"
is more exhausting than doing it myself.
Seems easier to just shut up and let her talk,
then let her do it all for me, anyway.

I wonder sometimes
if she knows that.

Schooling

When I was nine, I took horseback riding lessons.
My instructor, Debbie, imparted advice around a cigarette.
"Throw your heart over the fence," Debbie said.
"The horse will follow. Confidence.
Your horse responds to your body language."

Maybe this fake arm,
whom I have named Chuck,
is like a horse.
Practicing reaching for a book,
I visualize, stand tall,
then throw my heart over to the object,
hoping Chuck will follow.
Tilt forward at the waist,
shrug, open hand, pull back to shut.

As in riding,
the ideal doesn't always happen.
Sometimes the book slithers to the floor.
I want to whip something. Someone.
I have to walk around and breathe deep.
Chuck and I cool down, apart.

But as in riding,
sooner or later,
we saddle up
and try again.

Thought

Here's a question.
If we—
and by "we" I mean an amputee—
are supposed to be accepting,
unashamed of our new body,
unconcerned by gawks and furtive glances,
unfazed about blending,

then why are artificial hands crafted
to look so real?
There's "hair" on the "skin,"
half-mooned fingernails,
and wrinkles around the knuckles.
The labor involved
in painting a freckle,
an age spot on a silicone glove,
the money spent
on such artists to do such things
speaks to a desire
to melt
back into the blur.

Why don't they just come clean
instead of giving us
pamphlets about
self-image?

Different

If only Michael hadn't been so busy flirting his butt off with those stupid girls. He would have come in with you.

So?

Then it wouldn't have happened. Maybe the two of you together would have looked like too large a mass to be a seal or a fish or whatever, and the shark would have passed you by.

Or it might have been Michael.

Better him than you.

Oh, God, how can I even think such a thing? Stop it!

Your life would be so different right now.

He didn't come in. And it wasn't him. It was me. That's the way it is.

It could have been different.

I know.

It should *have been different.*

Albums

I run my hand
along the spines of the albums
lined across the shelves.
My finger rests on the plaid one.

Dad's last year.
I know all the pictures by heart,
and today, I'm in the mood to see his face.

But not

all those pictures

of the two-armed me.

His Voice

Justin called me today. "I miss you," he said.
Before I could tell him that I missed him more,

he was running like a faucet,
gushing about his friend Sam
and the LEGO set his grandparents sent him.
Something to do with Superman.

He didn't mention his leg at all.
Justin has other things on his mind.
Like life
and living it.

I miss his little face
and his skinny arms, too.

"Can I come over sometime?" he asks.
"I think I should come to *your* house,"
I say, trying to steady my voice.
"I need to meet this dog of yours.
Spot."
Justin laughs. "She's kissing me right now."

Justin laughing.
What a beautiful sound.

It Stinks

I see Mom cleaning,
cleaning,
washing and folding,
dusting. Shopping.

Guilt.

One afternoon,
while she is at work,
I try folding the laundry.
What a joke.
Wrinkled heaps, sleeves
poking sideways,
but at least Chuck is good for something—
he helps me get the shirts
on their hangers.

Taking out the trash,
I hold the bag at the top,
center,
but everything bulges out
and before I can reach the garage,
trash spills
to the ground.
Coffee grounds,
tin foil bits,
last night's spaghetti,

bread crusts—all
lie before me
like a dare.

Michael finds me
crying in the garage,
surrounded by mess.
"It's okay," he says
gently, and steers me inside.
"I'll take care of it."

I don't know what's worse.
Knowing I can't do something as simple
as take out the trash
or seeing my brother
feel sorry for me.

Perhaps Decaf

Rachel and I prep
for the expedition.
I try not to think
about how I felt
at the grocery store.
I try to be
a clean slate.

In my room,
I set my purse on the bed,
unzip it, fish out the wallet,
fumble around for money;
dollars wrinkle up in a wad,
coins tinkle to the floor.

"Try again," Rachel says.
And I do.
I use Chuck to help,
but frankly, Chuck
is a pain in the ass.
He clunks, bumps, and blocks
my view.
Chuck is removed from the scene.

Rachel raises an eyebrow.
"You're going without it?"

"No. Of course not.
But it's in the way," I say.

This time, I get the wad of money out,
lay it down,
extract three dollars,
set them aside.
I return the remaining bills,
somewhat crinkled,
to the pocket of the wallet.

Coins next,
raining, bouncing, thumping
off our freshly painted toenails.
Rachel draws her feet up to the bed,
fluffs up her bangs, and sighs.
"Maybe skip the change?"

"Right." I remove one more dollar.
I hand over the money. Rachel
scoops up some littered dimes and dumps them
into my palm.
I stare at the tiny coin pocket on my wallet.
Can't slide them in this way,
they'll fall to the sides.
To hell with it. I slide the coins into my pocket.
"Good enough," Rachel says.

I stand straight,
zip the purse shut.

"Order?" Rachel asks.
"Tall mocha latte, please," I reply.
Rachel pretends to hand me a cup,
then goes into her standard
Idiot Person
imitation, hunching apelike.
"Say, what happened to your arm there?"

I almost laugh, but this is a dry run.
"I had an accident," I say,
and practice becoming a distant
stone wall.
"Oooh, good look," Rachel says.
"That would shut *me* down.
But you may run into a real boob
out there. What if he or she does this?
'*Hey,* wait a sec, I know you.
You're that girl that—'"

"Okay, I want to stop now,"
I say quickly.

"'The shark girl!'"
Rachel crows, still in ape mode.
"'Hey, I saw that video on—'"

"Stop it, Rachel."
"'Wow, that must have been weird.
Do you remember anything that—'"

"Knock it off. No one will say that."

"'Did you *see* the shark?'"

"It's none of your damn business
and I would prefer you don't ask me
such personal questions!"

We stare at each other,
shocked.

Then Rachel smiles,
and she is herself again.
"Good. I think you're ready."

Chuck is strapped on.
The three of us set out
for the perfect cup of java.
My knees shake,
my armpits grow wet
when we enter the coffee shop,
teeming with bodies and voices,
the clatter of humanity over
the smell of espresso and shortbread,
we're onstage,

all the world is watching.
I've forgotten the script.
I grab Rachel's elbow.
"I can't do this. Let's go."

She shakes me off.

"Ten minutes," she whispers.
"We can last ten minutes.
That's all I ask."
For a second, I hate her.
With alarming passion.

Deep breaths, I think. She's right.
Ten minutes.
We can do it.
Waiting our turn,
I whisper my line once more,
for practice.
"Tall mocha latte, please."

My throat is so dry,
so tight,
I know one sip
will choke me.

Sipping

At a table barely big enough
for two cups and a scone,
Rachel and I sit.
We don't really talk.
I am watching the clock.
Feeling the pressure of
so many bodies, so much noise,
crushing.
Rachel seems nervous, too.
We smile thinly at each other,
and absorb.

Those girls over there,
tossing their heads
and jabbering away,

those two guys
sitting facing straight out
instead of toward each other,
talking,
laughing,

that woman reading a magazine,
sipping a chocolate drink
with cream on top
who looks at me briefly,

takes in the fake hand
and doesn't look again,

all of them
have no idea
how whole they are,
how beautiful
and dangerous
and fragile
they are,

and that
for this moment,
they are all
safe,
on dry land.

Failing Expectations

This very thing happened to someone else.
A girl, in Hawaii.
Her arm was taken completely off.

She was back surfing a month later.

Why can't I be like that?
I want to be like that. . . .
And I don't.

I suck.

Everyone wants me to be brave,
to impress them with dazzling fortitude,
to give them inspiration
and smiles and a feeling of,
If she *can do it, I can, too.*

Maybe the old
If she's *not complaining about life,*
then I won't, either.

Because then,
everyone else gets to say,
Looking at the Shark Girl, I realize—
I'm lucky.

Well, screw that.
Complain? Yeah. The pain,
for one thing. The tingling,
the numbness, the stupid chafing.
The hot prosthesis,
the stares, the inability to do
ANYTHING normally.

Some days, I hate everyone I see.
Even babies.

How's that for inspirational?

Back At It Again

I must love to punish myself.
I can't leave that
pad of paper alone.

The point of the pen
won't travel the path
I have planned.
It oozes out of a circle,
wobbles to the left,
wanders off
in midline.

I draw shaky ovals,
crooked squares,
while the lamp on my bedside table
patiently dries out my scalp.

Maybe I'll never get the shapes
precisely
the way I want.

Maybe
it's all just a big,
fat joke.

But I continue,
just in case.

Dear Jane:

My Uncle/Aunt/Brother-in-Law's Friend Had Their Leg/Foot/Toe/Finger or Hand Amputated Because of Diabetes/Frostbite/Circulation Problems/War/Job Injury, But You'd Never Know It, Because They Are So Funny/Athletic/Good-Natured/Spiritual/Successful/ At Ease with Themselves/Happy.

If I have to listen to one more story,
I will scream.

August 30

"Get out here, we've got lots to do."
Michael has the lawn mower
and clippers.
"Bring the trash can," he tells me.

I roll it over to the edge of the lawn.
Awkwardly, as with anything else.
I am not wearing Chuck for this;
Chuck is driving me insane with his clumsiness,
and besides, it is too damn hot to wear that thing.

"It's too damn hot," I say, trying Michael.
Maybe he'll be nice again.
Mr. Martinez is in his driveway,
washing his car. He waves. He watches.

But Michael is not nice; he is Michael.
"Stop whining," he says. "Now.
Welcome to the Arrowood school of gardening.
Today, we are going to learn how to
Mow the Lawn."
He spreads the words out like a proclamation:
Mow   the   Lawn.

"Michael, I don't want—"
"You don't have to thank me. First step,
start the mower."

He makes me turn the key and pump the red button,
press the black knob. The mower roars to life.
Mr. Martinez still watches.
Michael spreads his hands. "Begin."

I hate him. I hate Mr. Martinez for being in his driveway,
I hate the grass for growing, and the sun for being so hot.
I hate the mower, straining to the right like a live animal.
"Put your weight to the right," Michael calls.
My hand is cramped,
my legs rubberizing,
grass bits spatter my shorts,
sweat pours down into my underwear.

"I can't do this," I yell above the mower.
But Michael isn't even watching,
he's too busy clipping the edges,
calm as a fat cat.

I push the stupid mower around,
pretending the grass is Michael's face,
his smirk being chewed off bit by bit.
Mr. Martinez goes back to his car washing,
smiling with white teeth.

Later,
Michael says, "See? You can do this.
Next week, I'm off to college.
Time for you to make this your job."

Aching legs, aching back,
I shower the sweat away,
thinking he's right.
It sucked to mow the lawn.
But it would have sucked more
to see Mom pushing that mower each week.

And maybe,
it's kind of nice
for Michael to treat me
like old plain Jane.

Snip, Snip

Days skirting the issue.
The tangles in the comb,
that heavy dryer,
Mom's pinchy fingers trying to help.
Shouts of impatience,
bitten back. Walking around
looking like I just rolled out of bed.
Enough.

Rachel and I slip into the bookstore,
snatch up every hair magazine made,
which is about three too many.
We see Angie with her dad
in the checkout line.
"Jane? Rache? What are you guys doing?"

Great. It all comes out.
"You're not cutting off your hair,"
Angie states flatly.
She touches my ponytail.
"You've got the prettiest hair out of all of us;
you CAN'T cut it off. I forbid it."
She's joking, but not so much.
"Call me when you get home—we'll discuss this!"
She's off.
Rachel looks guilty.

Later,
I shake off the store clerk's stare,
pore over the magazine.
Lana, the hairdresser I get at the salon,
approves the torn-out picture I've brought.
"That'll bring out your eyes," she says,
"and it's easy to take care of."
I am grateful when she drops
the giant smock around me, hiding everything.
She starts cutting away as she talks.
"A dab of gel, run your fingers through each side,
bam, you're out the door. Love it."
Locks fall to the linoleum floor,
a litter of feathered casualties.
Emerging from beneath Lana's scissors
is a face. My face?
Too pale. Too serious. But there I am,
and I can't help but wonder
what Angie will say at school,
what *her* face will look like
when she sees
I defied her orders.

Opposite Sides of the World

"Be good," my brother says. His voice
rumbles in my ear as he hugs me.
"When you go back to school,
you'll be fine. Really."
His chin scratches across my cheek.
"Okay," I say, meaning to speak
loudly, but whispering instead.
I'm losing something.
Something more than Michael.

"Please call me when you get there,"
Mom says. Her knuckles are white
when she grips Michael's shirt.
"It's only UCLA, Mom," he says,
but Michael doesn't break the hug.
"I'll be coming home a lot."

Mom stands next to me, sniffling,
watching Michael climb into his truck.
I want to hug her,
but her shoulders say "stay away."
As Michael drives off, we both wave,
and though we're standing side by side,
we might as well be
on opposite sides of the world.

Buttons

Found a jar of buttons
in Mom's craft cabinet today.
I ask if I can have them.
Tiptoe into Michael's room,
breathe in the scent;
dirty sneakers,
cologne, and empty closet.

Underneath the "fast cars" calendar,
I sit, the buttons spread out on the dark carpet.
They clatter in miniature
when my hand stirs the plastic pile.

It grows dark while I
arrange and rearrange.
Funny how you can make a picture
without really thinking about it.
Everything shifts
with the removal of just one black button
or the two blues,
or the square white one
with the small red rose.

It's almost like sketching.

September: 8:33 p.m., Sunday

Hey, Rache.

Hi. Hang on, let me put the phone by the bed. Okay. How are you?

Oh, you know.

Nervous?

Uh, yeah. Just a little.

(Nervous laughter from both.) That was a dumb question.

Why don't you ride in with me tomorrow? Mom's driving me.

I can't; I have a dentist appointment at seven. Dad's driving me straight to school after.

Oh.

But I can meet you. By your locker. Or . . .

Yeah, okay.

Want to meet outside? By the bike rack?

Well . . . whatever.

Jane, I'm sorry. I can't get out of the appointment, though; my dad would kill me.

I know. (Long pause.)

Too bad Michael isn't there.

My *brother* Michael? What could he do?

I don't know. Beat up anybody who says anything. (More nervous laughter from both.)

Rachel, what are you going to wear?

My red top with the stripe. And my black pants. You?

I don't know. I was thinking about the top with . . . oh, who cares? Does it matter?

Of course it does. We might run into someone gorgeous. Like Max Shannon!

Yeah, well, no one is going to even see what I'm wearing. They'll be too busy checking out my nice fake arm. I could wear a bag over my head and no one would notice.

Oh, Jane! I feel so bad. I wish you wouldn't say that.

But it's true—you know it is. I'm going to wear my cosmetic arm all week. I can't wear the hook. Not right away. It's too .

Tomorrow will be the hardest. It'll be all downhill after that.

Maybe.

You should call Angie or Trina. They'd ride over with you.

Yeah, maybe I will.

Do it. Promise?

No.

(Loud sigh.) Come on, you don't have to do this alone.

I know. I have to go. Mom needs the phone.

Oh. Okay. Well . . . call Angie, all right?

Okay.

Jane?

What?

You can do this.

Lighted Numbers

The clock reads
midnight,
then one,
two,
three
a.m.

I'd rather go back
to that beach
and dip my toes
in the cold gray water,
than step into school

in just a few hours.

Drowning

I skip breakfast,
but throw up anyway.
On the ride over,
I have to pee so bad.

Oh, God, I can't do this.
What if I fall down?
Will I make people sick?
I don't think I can stand up.
My legs have turned to Jell-O.
But—
Here we are, pulling up,
Mom is waving good-bye,
and here I go, stepping out
into the current of beautiful,
two-armed classmates,
streaming into the building.

And now they are noticing me,
and now they are looking,
and now
the day begins.

Currents

Eyes stare,
dart away,
flit back again.
Rigid backs from those pretending
not to see.
Walking through the halls,

I am Moses,
parting the Red Sea.

I am a leper,
come to town.

I have the plague.

Whispers

That girl that got bitten by a . . .

Jane Arrowood. That girl who . . .

The one that . . .

. . . her arm off?
Partly off.
They had to amputate it, though.

My mother cried when she heard.
We barely know Jane.

We sent a card.

We sent flowers.

. . . and then the shark just . . . ?

Yeah.

I wanted to call her or visit or something.
But I never did.

I don't know what to say.

I'm never going to the beach again.

I Could Run Away, But Then What?

Angie and Trina find me at my locker.

"Oh, my God. You cut your hair?"
Angie asks.
Trina hugs me. "You look nice."
No one comments on my long sleeves
among their short ones.

"This cut—it's so different."
Angie is still on about my hair.
"I wish you'd taken *me* with you.
I could have given you a couple of tips."
My classmates pass, staring. Not
at my hair.

Or my sweater.

It's time for homeroom.

Shark Girl

Their heads lean toward each other.
Their whispers reach my ears.
The two girls over there
fingering their notebooks,
staring.

If they would lift their tinted eyelashes
they would notice I'm staring back.
But they don't.
So I turn in my chair,
placing my shoulder out of their sight.

Art Class

Students stream in,
pull iron stools up to the tall tables.
Mr. Musker puts a hand
on my shoulder. "I'm glad to see you, Jane.
How are you feeling?"

His tired face,
his hound dog eyes,
so familiar.

This room, too,
with its blend of odors: turpentine,
fixative, clay, and dust.
I shouldn't be here. It's like showing
a dead person her lost life,

and all
she missed.
It's cruel.

Pounding, thumping, rolling.
Everyone's hands pull,
like the surf.
Pottery wheels spin.
Clay becomes form.
I crumble pastels across
black paper,

listening to the slap slap of hands.
"Does this count a lot toward our final grade?"
Michele Lomer asks,
lobbing a wad of gum
inside her lower jaw
as she surveys her crooked urn.
Mr. Musker hurries over,
works with Michele's limp hands
upon the dusty clay,
but it's like trying to revive a corpse.

When the class ends, Mr. Musker beckons.
"Jane, how are you *really* doing?"

I want to tell him,
but it's too melodramatic.

Can't he see?
I'm like the pots
lined up by the kiln.

Half-finished.

The Hallway Encounter That Leaves Me
Weak in the Knees

Max Shannon rolls through the halls,
his hair still wet from senior swim team practice.
Frankenstein
slips from my hand.
Max Shannon stops,
rescues the book with slender fingers.

"You're that . . . uh, you're Jane, right?"
His tan cheeks turn pink.
"How's it going?"
His lips are perfect.
My face gets hot.

"You need help with that?"
He jerks his chin toward my backpack.
"No, I'm fine. Thanks."
His eyes seem magnetic.
"It's great you're okay.
My cousin lost her leg.
She switched to home school.
She was too embarrassed to leave the house."

"Oh."

Max's chin has a dimple.
"You're probably sick of questions.
Does anybody ask you about anything *else*?"

Angie and Rachel appear. They stare.

"What a stupid question!" Max smacks his forehead.
"Sorry, I'm an idiot.
Forget I bothered you."
He folds himself into the passing crowds.

Rachel raises her eyebrows. "Well!"
I laugh, but
Max wouldn't talk to me
if I was just me.
I shouldn't feel flattered, then.
Or happy.
Definitely not jelly-legged.
Angie doesn't smile like Rachel.
She just says, "Come on, we're going to be late."

Crap Overheard

"I heard she got tons of mail while she was in the hospital."

"I heard the president wrote to her."

"I heard they wanted to make a movie for television out of it, and her mom asked for too much money, so they didn't do it."

"I feel sorry for her."

"She was such a good artist."

"*Really* good."

"What do you think she'll do now? What would you do?"

"Probably kill myself."

"Shut up. You would not."

"Well, no. But God. What a nightmare. I would, like, have nightmares every night for the rest of my life."

"Did you see the video?"

"Yeah. You?"

"Yeah."

"Pretty sick."

"I want to talk to her, you know? Say something. But I don't know what."

"She would probably rather be left alone, anyway."

"Yeah. Probably."

Love

When I come home,
I can't wait to get Chuck
off of me, toss him onto the couch.
The whole day
is hot and heavy in my ears,
and I keep seeing faces in the hallways.

Walking to the kitchen,
I notice

flowers on the table. Sunflowers.
My favorite. A small square note
against the rippled glass vase:
I'm proud of you, Jane.
Love, Mom.

An e-mail from Michael:

```
UCLA has an awesome football team,
but even the fullbacks
aren't as tough as you are.
Hang in there. You can do it.
```

Exhaling, I realize
I can
    breathe
        again.

Dear Jane,

I am thirteen years old. I am a paraplegic. I had a skiing accident two years ago and now I have to be in a wheelchair. I intend to walk again someday, even though my doctors tell me I won't.

I know how it is to feel different. I just wanted to tell you that it does get easier, and if your friends are good friends, they'll stick by you and not make a big deal out of the way you look or whatever. I hope you have good friends. I hope things are going okay for you. It helped me to talk about it to my friends, but after a while, I didn't want to talk about it anymore. I just wanted to get back to doing normal things, which isn't always easy, but I think if you are willing to work hard, you can find a way to do anything.

Good luck with everything,
Riley

Again

I wake up, crying.
Again.
The smell of the sea,
the roar of water in my ears,
screaming. Cold, black rush,
a gray blur of flesh,
a single black eye.
My legs barely carry me
to the bathroom,
where I vomit.

Back in bed,
I wait,
watching for pink sky.

Bumped Off

Angie spies me standing,
backpack skewed,
staring at the bulletin board.
First prize, one hundred dollars,
blue ribbon, and modest fame.
Angie walks up.
Alongside me,
she reads the notice.

"Oh, yeah, the art contest
is coming up." She pauses.
"You've won three years
in a row, right?"

"Yes."

She sighs. "Well. I wonder
who will win this year?"

The simple question
holds me at knifepoint,
breathless.

Angie puts an arm around me.
"Don't feel bad, Jane.
Besides, if you work hard,
I'm sure you will get it all back.

Right? You can enter next year,
as a senior."

No.
It's *my* contest.
It's *my* win.
Art is *my* thing. Now,
someone new
will climb the peak,
cast their shadow on
That Girl Who Got Bit by a Shark,
lying like so much flab; useless,
foolish.

Whoever she is,
she will be surrounded,
she will be in light,
she will be carried on a wave
of love and goodwill.

She will not know what it's like
to take up
unjustified space

in the universe.

LEGO Man

Justin and I
have hooked up for a playdate.
At his house, his parents
give me hugs, the dog
Spot licks my face,
my hand, my knee;
Spot is eager to be friends.
She presses close, tail thumping
when we sit at the table
and Justin shows me his LEGOs.

"I built this castle once."
He shows me the picture
in the "ideas" booklet.
"And this tower thing?
My dad and I made that last week."
He slides the booklet aside.
"We can't keep them, though;
otherwise we don't have enough LEGOs
to build anything else.
We *always* take them apart."

He states this firmly as
he digs out red rectangles,
black squares, and offers them
to me. "Let's build something."

If Justin were my brother,
I would buy him all the LEGOs
in the world, so he would never,
ever
have to destroy his creations.
I want to tell him this.
Instead I say,
"I'm not good at LEGOs."

Justin replies, "Sure you are."

We click and snap the pieces together,
discovering as we go
what it is we are making.

"How is school?" I ask.

"Fine."

"Do the kids . . . you know.
Do the kids . . ."

He looks up at me. "Make fun of me?"

"Yes." I study his face
while Spot sniffs my shoe.

"No. Well, one did.
But I don't care. Everyone else
treats me the same as usual."

"Good."

He hands me a blue LEGO.
"Do the kids make fun of *you*?"

I shake my head.
"Not really," I say, wanting to add
but of course, they stare.
Justin would understand staring.
He understands a lot of things my friends
don't, can't, never will.
"Do you like your new leg?" I ask.
He is not wearing it today.

"Yeah, it lets me do stuff.
Sometimes it kind of hurts, though."
He examines the LEGO creature
we hold between us. "Needs more black."

I blurt,
"I don't like my new arm."

"Is that why you're not wearing it?"
he asks.

I nod, and finger my pinned-up sleeve.
I can be armless with him,
natural and comfortable.

Justin scrabbles in the LEGO bucket.
He says,
"Have you drawn me a picture yet?"

"Um, no."
"Why?"
"Well, it's just not going well."

He looks into my eyes, kindly.
"It's okay. Keep trying."

Then he grabs the LEGO monster,
which is multicolored, tall and jutting,
and he makes a growling sound.
"ROAAARRRR."
We laugh.
"Let's play some computer games,"
Justin says.
Grabbing his crutches, he leads the way.
I follow,
wondering why
he seems like the big kid
and I

the small one.

Mr. DeLandro

In biology, Mr. DeLandro says,
"Next week we will be dissecting—
or in the case of some of you guys—*hacking up*—goldfish."
He winks at me. "Sorry, Jane, I couldn't get hold of a shark."

I could kick him. But I wait until after class,
swallow my thumping heart,
and step up to his desk.

"That remark you made—"

"Oh, I was just kidding around, you know that, right?"

"It wasn't funny."

"I apologize, Jane.
I was trying not to pussyfoot around your condition.
I thought it would make things easier on you."

"It didn't. I don't need help
and I *don't* need to be laughed at."

The price of confrontation? All day,
all that hot, restless night,
I try to forget the coldness in Mr. DeLandro's eyes,
the anger, white,
around his lips.

Thanksgiving

Happy Thanksgiving, sweetheart!

Hi, Aunt Karen! Happy Thanksgiving to you.

I sure wish we were together.

Me, too.

We have a houseful, though. Your grandparents are
here and Margie and her husband and my cousin's family.
There's seventeen of us! We sure have a lot to be
thankful for *this* year.

We do?

Well, *yes,* honey, we're all going to say a special prayer of
thanks that you are with us today, alive and well!

Oh.

Do you know I made a vegetarian stuffing in your
honor? I found the recipe when I was out there, in one
of your cookbooks!

That's great.

Hold on, your uncle Ben wants to get on the phone.

Janie?

Hi, Uncle Ben.

How are you?

I'm fine.

How's school? You never answered my e-mail about that.

It's fine.

We sure can't wait to have you out here at Christmas. You—

Janie?

Grandma?

Janie, I'm going to get off the phone and let you and your grandma talk, okay? We love you.

Bye. Hi, Grandma.

Hi, sweetheart, how are you?

I'm fine.

Did you help your mom put dinner together?

Um, not really.

Jane, why not?

Well, it's just us and two of her friends from school. She could handle it.

That's not the point, honey. You love to cook. You should be in there making your chocolate pie. Everyone would have loved it.

Well.

Besides, even if it's a small group, your mom shouldn't have to do it alone.

Would you like to talk to Michael? He's home for the weekend.

In a minute. Now listen, honey, I'm not trying to nag, but you need to get back into your routine. Your mom said you're not drawing, you're not cooking, you're not going out with your friends. She's making excuses for you, but I think you're not pushing yourself enough. What do you do when you come home from school?

I have homework.

You used to do homework *and* lots of other stuff.

Okay, okay, I don't want the silent treatment, you stubborn thing. You know I love you, Jane, right?

Mmm-hmm.

I'm just trying to help. You can't sit around forever.

I'm not sitting around! How can you say that?

I just meant I'm worried about you being in a depression.

Well, I do have a lot to be depressed about, you know.

I didn't mean you didn't. I just—

Janie?

Uncle Ben?

What in the world is going on here? Your grandma is all red in the face. Are you two fighting? On Thanksgiving?

No. She was just giving me some advice.

Do you need advice?

NO.

Are you sure? You want me to come out there and set you straight? I better not hear any bad things about my favorite niece.

I'm your *only* niece.

Your grandma is worried about you. Your mom is worried about you. We all just want you to be happy, okay?

No one needs to worry about me. I'm *fine*.

All right. Listen honey, put your mom on, okay? I want to say hello before we sit down to eat.

Okay.

Love you, Janie.

Bye.

Friday after Thanksgiving

"See you later, alligator."
Mom heads out for shopping.
Michael sleeps the day away
while I
lift every clock, photo, and scrap of paper
from every table, dresser, and shelf.
Lemon-scented polish,
the damp rag makes a dark slash through the dust.
Every item returned to its shiny home,
and then it's the heavy vacuum,
maddening in its complacent
refusal to cooperate. I wonder if it's friends
with the lawn mower. Soon, I am exhausted,
but the floor is done.

Folding laundry is a joke. But I can
peel sheets from the bed,
traveling from one side to the other,
then stuff them into the wash, one-handed,
unscrew cap, pour in suds of neon blue,
listen to the gurgle of a machine well fed.

Mom comes home,
crushes me in a hug.
"Thank you, honey. This is a nice surprise."

I sit in the chemical cleanness,
breathing the works of my labor,
feeling tired in a good way,
knowing this nice surprise
needs to become, once again,
my weekly obligation.
Not just for Mom,
but for both of us.
Because saying "I can't"
isn't going to cut it
when I'm living alone.

I think about calling Grandma to gloat.
But I hold off,
savoring instead
the quiet hum of the dryer,
clothes spinning inside.

Finding

Use of a hip
to pin one strap down,
plus some creative wiggling
makes putting on a bra
possible.
I can now deal with maxi pads
and their "wings"
fairly well.
Tying shoes?
Still a problem.
But,
I can button and zip
all by myself.
I've even made my own
bowl of cereal
twenty-two mornings in a row now.

Inch by inch,
centimeter by centimeter,
I gain back pieces
of lost ground.

Shopping

After art, I swing by Mrs. Guiano's desk.
She's our guidance counselor extraordinaire.
"Jane." She hugs me long, smelling of vanilla,
her glasses on a chain, crushed between us.

"I want to talk about nursing," I hear myself say.
I sit and listen to myself, tentatively, edge of my seat,
watching how myself will unfold this event.
"I want to know what classes I could take now
that will help me if I go into nursing school later.
Or physical therapy. Art therapy. Something like that."

Mrs. Guiano sits back as though I've just announced
I have a cure for cancer.
Stunned melts into thrilled.
"You come back,"
she says, flipping open her calendar and scribbling in it.
"I will have a stack of information waiting for you
after the holiday break. Classes, schools, careers,
you name it."

I hurry off, still smelling of vanilla from our hug.
I must not be so empty, after all.
A presence has dripped into my being—
something
that might be
excitement.

Max

Spies me hurrying along,
says:
"Can I help you with your books?"
I
say:
"Uh."
He takes the books to my locker,
hands them over with a smile.
Heads swivel our way.

The rest of my day is spent
conjugating numerous other,
better
replies
than
"Uh."

Tape

Wrapping presents is,
as my book on being handicapped urges me to say,
a *challenge*.
Not
a @#%&! pain in the ass.
NOT
a cause for smashing this room to pieces.

I'll ask Rachel to help me.
Then I'll ask Mom to help me with Rachel's.
But I won't cry in frustration,
no way.
It's Christmas.

Opening Presents

Mom likes the robe I got her,
holds the pink softness to her face,
smiles at me,
holds that smile.
I see a shine of tears
when she bends to
fold it back up.

Grandma serving up cinnamon rolls,
urging us to eat just one more;
Grandpa yawning, scratching his head,
an unopened gift in his lap,
slippers half off,
reaches out, squeezes my hand.

Michael in his gray wrinkled
sweatpants, gathering
balled-up wrapping paper,
flipping it into the fireplace,
asking "When is dinner?"
Already, even though it's early.
"I like a boy with an appetite,"
Grandma says, and hands him
another roll.
"Mother, you'll make us all fat,"
Mom groans, but she reaches
for the corner of the last roll

at the same time I do.
She catches my eye,
and we smile again.

Among the candles,
the Christmas tree lights,
and the sight of Mom
picking her way over
boxes of opened gifts,
a sudden rush fills me.
I'm here.
I'm alive, and I'm here.

Seems like tears of joy
should flow right about now.
Instead, I just smile,
lean back into the couch,
and enjoy the happiness,
deep and warm.

Hello, is this Jane Arrowood?

Yes.

This is Missy Howard. I am the vice president of programming for ABC. I wanted to talk to you about appearing on *Good Morning America.*

What?

Jane, we are so in admiration of you here. We know what you have been going through must be rough.

And you admire that?

Sorry?

I don't want to be on your show.

Now, Jane, hear me out. If you would be willing to come to New York, we would be glad to pay your way, and you and your family could make a vacation out of it. We could talk about—

No, thank you.

Jane, the whole nation saw your story on the news. People were shocked by what they saw. We know for a fact there are many, many people in our country who would love an update on you. How you're doing, how you are adjusting, what life is like now. People really do care, and I'm sure they would like to see you on television.

No, I—

I mean, this is your chance to leave an impression on everyone, isn't it? You don't want to be remembered as how you were seen in that video, do you? You want a chance to show everyone the human side of yourself, not just the story side, right?

I—

How does next Friday sound? We'd fly you and your parents out, of course, and—

No. I said no. I don't want to be on your show and that is final.

But—

Don't call here ever again.

After Slamming Down the Phone

Jane? Honey, what was that all about?

That was some stupid TV show. They wanted me to come on there and talk about myself.

What show?

Good Morning America.

Really? Well, honey, that's not some show. That's big.

Mom! Are you going to start, too? Do you *want* me to be on it?

Of course not. Why are you so upset? Jane, you're crying. Come here, honey.

She was so rude. She made it sound like I owed it to everyone to say I'm okay. Like people care? Everyone has forgotten about it.

The media doesn't fool around with forgotten people, dear. I'm sure there's a grain of truth in what she said. Don't look at me like that—I'm not saying she's right. I'm not saying you should be on the show. I'm just saying, you did get all those cards and letters. I mean, some of them are still coming.

I don't want them. I never asked for any of this. I don't owe anyone anything.

I know.

I hate this. I just want to be left alone.

Hm.

What. What are you thinking about?

Nothing.

What? Tell me.

Well. I don't know why, but I was just thinking about you and your art. About all those contests you're always winning. Do you remember in fourth grade when you won the blue ribbon for best artist of the year, and had to stand in front of an assembly and have your picture taken?

Yeah.

You loved that. You took a little bow and everything. They had to push you off the stage when you were done.

So?

You've always loved winning those things. You've always been the best artist in school, and you've been so proud of yourself in that department.

So?

It's just funny how we can crave attention in some areas of our life, but hate it in others.

I don't *crave* attention.

Not over this, of course not.

I don't *crave* any attention, ever.

Honey, we all do. Especially when we're young.

Mom! You make me sound so egotistical.

You're not. I'm not saying that. But if I were, it would be a very shared human trait. We all have egos, dear.

Have you been seeing Mel again?

No. But Jane, when are you going to draw again?

I don't know.

I think you are neglecting an important part of yourself.

You *have* been seeing Mel.

I don't need to see Mel to know how important your art is to you. I *am* your mother.

What's the point? I will never be able to make a living at it.

I don't agree. And besides, is that what it comes down to? You only want to create things to get paid?

Mom . . . I don't want to talk about this.

Of course not. You don't talk to me about anything anymore.

Mom . . .

I know, I know. You're a teenager. Everyone said to expect this. But I'm here, okay? If you need me?

I don't want to be on that show.

I understand.

If anyone else calls here, or they call back, tell them NO. Okay?

Okay.

Midnight at the Drafting Table

Forget the competitions.
I won't be able to even *enter*
this year, or maybe ever again.
A professional? Doubtful.
My days of "look at me"
are over.

As to why I didn't tell Mom
Yes, I've been working at it,
I don't know.

This thing is private,
very private,
and no one needs to stand witness
with a stopwatch or progress chart.
No one needs to say the wrong thing.

Door closed, I work at the drafting table.
Pen in hand,
pawing.

Something is not right in me
and won't be
until I can do this.

T·H·R·E·E

Storm Watch Tuesday

Tuesday it storms. A real
spring storm, common in March.
By the evening,
the freeways are flooded.
With fevered excitement,
the newscasters discuss the flooding,
the mud slides, the road closures.
As it grows dark,
Mom calls on her cell phone.
"I'm stuck on the 405.
It'll be another hour,
at least."
"Be careful," I tell her.

In the kitchen, I listen to the rain pounding the roof
and my stomach growling
as I poke through the cupboards.
I reach for the mini-wheats, then stop.
A plate of steaming scrambled eggs,
fluffy,
and buttered toast.
My favorite meal. I used to fix it all the time.
That's what I want.

Getting out the pan is no trouble.
But cracking the eggs is a problem.
The first one shatters on the edge of the bowl,

slops everywhere,
while the bowl scoots away from the impact.
It takes a long time to wipe the glop up.
I think about quitting.

The second egg splits open and falls into the bowl,
along with several shards of shell.
I pick them out, one by one, then rinse my fingers.
Egg number three goes in better —
there's only two fragments of shell to remove.
I add milk, which dribbles onto the counter,
then put the bowl against my stomach,
pin it against the wall with my weight,
and beat the eggs with a whisk.

Into the pan, the eggs crackle in hot butter.
I put two fat slices of cranberry bread
in the toaster. Get out a plate and a cup.
Spill the orange juice and swear.
Why is pouring stuff so weird?

I wipe it up,
hurry to stir the smoking eggs, check the toast,
stir the eggs again.
Tipping them onto a plate, half the eggs tumble
onto the counter.
A small portion falls on the floor.
Mabel snatches a piece, burns her mouth.
I try not to scream.

Buttering the toast is tricky.
I can't get the knife to spread the way I want,
just stab holes in the bread as it cools.

Mabel sits under my chair,
watching for falling crumbs.

The eggs are overcooked.
The toast is a buttered murder victim.
But I'm proud, really proud,
like I just had a baby or something.
I turn on the radio
and light the flowered candle on the table.
A victory dinner, as rain pours down outside.
"I did it," I tell Mabel,
who wags, ears pricked.
"I cooked dinner. Can you believe it?"

And next time will be easier, I think.

And the next time, and the next time.

I give Mabel a chunk of toast
and eat,

humming with the radio.

Rain

Mom gets home late.
She's carrying a bag from McDonald's. "For us!"

"I already made myself some eggs," I tell her.
I can see she's thrilled,
but trying not to gush.
"That's wonderful, honey."

Then I remember.
I forgot to wash the dishes.
Shit.

How am I going to scrub encrusted
dried egg
off a pan
with one hand?

"I'll wash up," Mom calls from the kitchen.
"You sure you don't want some fries?"

Will Mom go to college with me?
Live in my apartment,
wash the dishes for me?

I walk into the kitchen
and start the hot water.
"I said I'd get those," Mom says.

I pick up the messy egg pan,
plunk it into the sink.
"No, I got it." I look at her for a minute.
Mom hesitates, then takes her food
out to the living room.

I pick up the scrub brush,
and begin.

Cup

Progress? Yes. I think.
I mean, that thing
there definitely resembles a paw.
That, a fish.
And the horse,
well, at least its legs are connected
with the ground line.
But the faces? Skewed, shifty;
lifeless eyes.

When I sketch
the lumpy, bumpy things that are animals,
I can feel love—
joy,
hovering, dangling,
over my cup.

If only I could create a pair of eyes
to look back into mine.
Then maybe,
the cup
would fill up.

Our Story

This is how it could go.
Max will ask me out.
Somewhere quaint,
like the aquarium perhaps.
We'll eat vanilla ice cream
while watching squid probe.

At the shark tank
he will suddenly realize
we shouldn't be anywhere
near a shark tank.

By the flounder, our hands touch.
In the jellyfish room,
our shoulders brush,
a manta ray drifts past
and we turn to each other—
he'll kiss me
while giant red crabs
scale pink coral behind thick glass,
and crowds of people shuffle by,
consulting guidebooks.

Maybe I'll cry.
"I'm so different, Max.
Can this work?"
He'll take my face in his hands,

his skin blue from the fish lights,
and say,
"Don't you get it? I love you
because of who you are *inside*."
Tears.
Embrace.
I discover I always wanted
to be a ballerina;
Max wins a swim scholarship
to Harvard.
"We'll always have the kelp forest, Max."

Happy ending, roll credits,
pick our way out, over
crushed pieces of popcorn,
to emerge
into the glaring light of day.

Opinions, Over Tuna

At lunch one day,
I tell them about the phone call
a few weeks ago, the one
from the TV station.

Rachel is horrified.
Trina repulsed.
Elizabeth stares.
Angie speaks up.

"*Why* did you say no?"
She waves her sandwich
around as she talks.
"You could have had a free trip
to New York.
They would have given you
a makeover, maybe.
New clothes or something.
You could have seen a play.
You could have had a lot of fun!"

"By being on display?"
Rachel demands.

Angie rolls her eyes.
"Jane. Did you ever think
that maybe you would do someone

some good
by talking about your story?"

Elizabeth jumps in.
"I was thinking the same thing."
She shrugs apologetically.
"There may be a lot of other kids out there
like you. Or that boy
you talk about, Justin.
Maybe if they could see you,
they'd feel better."

"Why? Because I'm doing so great?"
I ask, sounding totally old and sour.
I try again.
"I mean, what can I say
that is so inspirational? It's because
of doctors I survived. Now I just . . .
I don't know. I just go on."

"Yeah, but you're high profile,"
Trina adds. She shrugs, too.
"Not that I'm saying you should do it.
I'm just saying."

We wait.
"Saying what?" I ask.

Trina digs into a bag of chips.

"I don't know. Nothing."

Rachel gives me a look,
a *Don't listen to them,
you did the right thing*
look.

That is why Rachel
is my best friend.

Just Say It . . .

Angie: "Jane, you might want to try mascara.
Why don't you wear mascara?
Mascara would help your eyes stand out.
You should wear your makeup . . ."

Different.

Angie: "You need something with a V-neck.
Turtlenecks make your chin look big."

Different.

Angie: "You could use a shoe with a heel, too.
And have you thought about wearing more silver?
It might make you look less pale. You'd look . . ."

Different.

In her eyes,
everything about me that has always been me
isn't good enough—
anymore.

Playground

Justin and I hook up again,
which is not easy,
because every time I call
he's going over to a friend's house.
But today, we're here.
Side by side,
we walk two blocks from his house
to a playground. It reminds me
of walking the hospital halls with
Justin in his wheelchair, beside me.
He's come a long way.

Justin steps along steadily
on his leg,
only swaying slightly,
but he is careful
when we pass over uneven
breaks in the sidewalk.

"Sometimes I still fall down,"
he explains. "But not much."

At the park, rocking on swings,
a spring breeze whispering,
Justin tells me that he is
playing softball with his friends,
in a league, even.

"They give me extra time to run the bases,"
he says. He sighs. "But I still
get out sometimes." He leans back,
pulling his weight against the chains
of the swing. "But that's okay.
I'm getting really good at hitting."

I can't bear the image.
What kind of idiot kid
tags out someone who
can barely run? Don't they care?

Justin breezes on. "I want to play
soccer again. With my friends.
My dad and I
are working on it.
He may take me to the World Cup
for my birthday."

Good job, Justin's dad. Way to go.

I drag my toes through the wood chips
beneath us. Spot, tethered to a tree,
rolls on her back.
"By the way. When is that?" I ask.

"The cup?"
"No, your birthday."

"May 28. Are you
going to buy me a present?"

"Of course. What would you like?
More LEGOs?"

"No. I have lots of those.
Let me think. Hmm."

I wait. Then I wait some more.
Justin, swinging, with half his
leg gone forever,
a prosthesis that still causes him to trip,
and soccer just out of reach,

can't think of one thing
he wants for his birthday.

Which is why I love you, Justin.
So much.

March 16, Sixteen

Physical therapy followed by
icy cold lattes at Starbucks,
a hot cinnamon scone to share,
Mom's lipstick left on the rim of her cup.
Her wrist flicks
as she checks the time.
"Got a date?" I joke,
but she just shakes her head at me,
with a wistful smile. "Seems only yesterday
I walked you to kindergarten."

We come home,
Mabel barking in the dark,
and there
in the corner, a massive lump,
impossibly shaped.

"Surprise!"
Rachel, Angie, Trina, Elizabeth
explode from behind the sofa,
leap from the kitchen doorway;
my knees buckle,
a flash goes off.
"You should have seen your face!"
"Were you surprised?"

"Happy Birthday!"

Don't Say Cheese

The surprise party launches
full swing into gossip
and Cheetos.
Mom has her camera out;
I corner her quick.
"No pictures, Mom."

"But this birthday is special."
She lifts the camera again. "Please?"
"No, really."
Her lip trembles. "Jane. Back
in the hospital,
I thought—"
Mom's face wrenches suddenly
and she whispers,
"I thought you wouldn't live
to see this day.
I thought I'd be visiting
your grave . . ."
Cheetos poised,
everyone stares
as I put my arm
around my sniffling mom.

I get everyone together for a photo,
but I stand
in the back.

Gift

Angie gives me a makeup kit.
All purples, all *not* my colors.

She wants so much for me to transform
to someone new, someone more like her.

Can't she see I'll never be like her,
whole and pretty and normal?

Can't she see?

Different, Again

If only this had never happened. You would be doing so much more right now.

I'd be drawing normally.

Yes!

I'd be driving. Dating. Maybe working at a paid job.

Your whole life would be normal. THIS is not normal.

Stop.

Your life is so different now.

It is what it is.

It's not fair, and it won't ever be the same.

I know.

It should have been different.

I know.

Different.

Hospital Help

Lindsey is thrilled at my request.
"We would *love* to have you
as a volunteer."

I fill out papers,
attend training.
Then I'm ready to go.
Saturdays, nine to twelve.

Drop-Off

"You really want to do this, Jane?
These are your *Saturdays*
we're talking about."

"It's not like I have a lot going on,
Mom. And yes, I really
want to do this."

"Your little outfit is cute."

"Thanks."

"I'll pick you up at twelve."

"If we start my driving lessons soon,
I can drive myself eventually."

"Um. Yes."

"Wouldn't that be good?"

"Yep. All right, see you later."

"Bye."

Burned into My Mind

Inside the hospital walls
everything comes back;
suddenly,
I think
I've made a terrible mistake.
I can't breathe here.
The hallways, the food trays,
the noises of phones and medical
blips and beeps. . . .
When I see the door to the room
that was mine,
a wave of ice washes over me.

Lightheaded, I take refuge
in the restroom
before I'm ready to try again.

But seeing the faces
when I deliver flowers
helps.
Lindsey's thumbs-up as she flashes past
does, too.
Mel drops by, for a hug,
with a shining smile.
"Good for you, Jane.
Good for you."

The thing that helps
most of all
is remembering how it felt
to be here
and how much the people
around me
made a difference.
Isn't that what I wanted, after all?
To make a difference?
I check my palm,
pressing it against my cheek.
Cold.
But useful in delivering get well cards,
filling water pitchers.

So, I get on with it,
trying to make a difference.

Dear Jane,

I am writing to tell you that I hope you get well soon. It must be difficult to recover from such a loss, but I am told it is possible. I myself have lost the use of my left arm due to a recent stroke, and I can sympathize with what you must be going through. Many things I loved to do I can no longer do, or at least, not as easily. Life is funny, and sometimes it's easy to question why terrible things happen to good people, especially young folks like yourself. I believe there is a reason, though we may not see it for a long time. My hope for you is that someday, you feel that this accident has not ruined your life; only changed it from the original plan.

As I work through my physical rehabilitation, I will think of you, going through the same. I wish you the best.

Courage,

Andy

Tools

A big cardboard box arrives
Saturday afternoon.
Stuff I ordered off the Internet,
from a specialty site.
Michael, home for the weekend,
carries the box inside,
cuts it open with a knife.
Together,
we dig through the contents.

"The Unskru jar opener,"
he says, holding the object aloft.
We stare at the spelling a moment.

"Bolt it underneath the cabinet,"
I explain, fishing another object
from the box.
"Then I can slide the jar into the slot
and twist it open."
"For all your mayonnaise needs,"
Michael says.

"Oh, shut up." I pull out the special knife,
resembling an arc,
the blade curved and shining,
the handle round, straight, and fat.
At last. I can chop, or slice a sandwich,

without making such a mess.
"Hey, that's pretty cool,"
Michael says, reaching for the knife.
"I want one of these."

At the bottom, among Styrofoam peanuts,
lies a cutting board.
Michael holds it up,
turning it over in his hands.
"There's a lip," I point out,
touching it with my little finger.
"You can hook it
to the edge of the counter."
Two "feet" at the edge
keep the cheese
or the whatever
from sliding off the board.

There's also a white mixing bowl
that will not slip.

"Well, aren't you all set,"
Michael says. He gathers up
the scattered packing bits.
"You can go back to cooking for us.
Please.
Before Mom kills us all."

Fingering my new tools,
I think about the people
who devote their lives
to inventing stuff like this.
Things that make life
a bit easier.
I wonder who they are

and why they invent things like this

and if they ever hear the words

"thank you."

Wheels

"I still need to learn to drive."

"I know, honey."

"I'm going to start saving for a car soon.
A used one. You know that."

"Yes, I do."

Neither of us mentions
we can't imagine what I'll do for employment
to save for this imaginary car.
The issue is independence.

"Michael bought a car."
"Yes, he did."
"If you're not going to teach me, can I ask him to do it?"

"Jane. Do we have to rush it?
You're still getting used to your new hand . . ."

"An electric hand has nothing to do
with me learning to drive.
I might as well learn to drive without it,
don't you think?"

Mom nods, but remains sitting,

plucking at a hole in the couch.
"I guess we could go out this weekend."

"Why not now?"
"Because it's dark."
"So?"
Sigh. "Jane, I don't want to."

In my room, I hear her call,
"You don't need to slam your door,
you know. I said we'd go
this weekend."

I need to know how to do this
now.
My friends
are practicing parallel parking already.

They know
they are days from freedom.
I need to know that, too.

Hello

Tonight,
the face of a fox
emerges beneath my hand.
Without warning
his slanted eyes
lock onto mine.
A face, there all along,
coming sharply into focus.
Real eyes.
Eyes!
Alive.

My heart beats faster.
I want to shout,
wake up the entire house,
the neighborhood, everyone.
Instead, I only wake up Mabel,
who blinks sleepily from the bed
as I dance around the room.

Synchronicity

I missed the bus,
because I was talking to Mrs. Guiano
about nursing school
and didn't want the conversation to end.
I start walking home
with all my books
in the crook of my arm.
Halfway down Raymond Avenue, the wind picks up.
Bits of dead leaves skip around my ankles;
this reminds me of children dancing,
and I wonder
if I could plan some kind of party
for the kids at the hospital.
I don't know what kind,
but those kids could use some fun.

A red car passes, slows down,
then reverses.
I put my head down and walk fast,
grateful that there's a woman across the street,
sweeping out her garage.
She'll be the witness in case I am assaulted.
The guy in the car sticks his head out.
"Jane? Can I give you a ride?"

Max Shannon himself.

The Ride

"You thought I might assault you?"
Max throws back his head and laughs.
"Not *really,*" I say, and I'm laughing, too.
"I mean, I'm alone, this car stops and backs up . . ."
"Right. What else could it possibly mean
but that I'm a psychotic animal?"
There's a tiny nick under his jaw,
maybe from shaving.
Max stops at a red light,
reaches over and plucks a book from the stack in my lap.
"The Call of the Wild?" he says.
"I liked *White Fang* better."
He places the book back on the stack
with care. "I can bring it in for you, if you want."

Though I've read it, I say, "That would be great."
Max drums his fingers on the steering wheel.
"I just realized.
This would go a lot better if you tell me where you live."
I give him directions,
wishing I could send him on some long, winding route
that would take a couple of days to complete.
But we're almost home.
"Are you ever going to come to a swim meet?" he asks.
"We don't get a lot of fans. The team could really use the
    cheering."
"I'll come to the next one," I blurt.

Could I sound any more eager?
"Great." He smiles. "Hey, how come you're not on the bus?"

He listens as I tell him about Mrs. Guiano and
medical school.
"That is totally cool," he says. "You'd make a great nurse.
Or a doctor."
"I've also been looking at occupational therapy," I tell him.
"There's so much that's looks interesting."
As he smiles and nods, I realize what I just said.
So *much* that looks interesting?
Wow.
Just a few months ago,
my radar was EMPTY.

So it's true, then?
Time makes a difference?
Who knows.
Time is still passing.

The Scoop

"Mom was driving me and Angie to the mall
and we passed you in Max's car!"
Rachel sounds gleeful.
"Gimme the scoop."
I tell her about the nick under Max's jaw,
about *White Fang,*
the way his car smelled like oranges,
everything.

Angie calls.
She gushes, she fusses,
she says:
"But,
I heard
he's with Megan Dalloway now."

Soaking in the bathtub later that night,
I wonder how Angie can call to tell me that,
and still call
herself
a friend.

Overheard

Emily Morrison says:
"He only talks to her because he feels sorry for her.
It's not like she's pretty or anything."
Behind my locker, I watch
Emily's enormous feet pass, and
the girl she's with, someone new,
says,
"Can you imagine getting your arm bitten off
by a *shark*?"

As though getting your arm bitten off by a lion
would be easier to live with.
They're both idiots.

So why am I the one
feeling stupid?

Lightbulb

I got it.
I know just what to get
Justin for his birthday.

I think,

I hope,

he'll love it.

That Ship Has Sailed

Max. I want his arms, around me.
That smile, that shine in his eyes,
when he looks at Megan,
I want that for me. Us. Together.

Rachel states:
"You don't even know him. You're creating fantasy."
Trina adds:
"He is probably an excessive nose picker,
or kicks his dog around when he goes home."

But Elizabeth says:
"Maybe not. Maybe he's every bit
as wonderful as he seems.
Sexy, cute, smart, athletic . . .
maybe I'm in love with him, too, Jane.
Can we share him?"

We laugh, and bump shoulders.
But I wish there was a grain
of hope, a toehold somewhere with Max.
When I think of his hands
and I think of his eyes,
it's like watching a boat sail away,
white sails growing ever smaller,
leaving me
on an empty shore.

Maybe

Maybe if you were normal-looking, Max would actually like you, instead of feel sorry for you.

He doesn't feel sorry for me.

Everyone feels sorry for you.

They do not.

If only this hadn't happened. None of this crap would be going on. You'd feel normal. Remember normal?

I think so.

Maybe you'll never feel that way again.

Stop.

If only that shark had been swimming anywhere else that day. Anywhere.

Anywhere else.

Anywhere.

Leagues

Angie and I walk through the halls;
I'm going to art,
she's going to English.
"Anyway," she is saying, "I have
to tell you. I think Matthew
has a crush on you."

"Matthew from science class?"
Angie nods, glowing.
"Uh-huh. Have you noticed the way
he finds reasons to talk to you lately?
About homework and stuff?"

"Yeah, but that's about homework."

"I don't think so. I saw him *looking* at you
a couple of times this week. I think
he may ask you out."

We reach art class and pause
at the doorway.
"I doubt it."

Angie sighs. "Jane, you can't
hold out for Max, you know."

Stung, I fall back on pretense.
"Huh? Who says I am?"

Angie leans against the doorjamb,
lowering her voice as students
squeeze past us.
"Come on. I know you're, like,
in love with him. But he's with Megan.
And he's kind of out your league."

"Thanks a ton."

"*My* league, too," Angie says,
hurt, confused.
"I'm not saying it has anything to do
with your arm, so don't go there.
I just meant, he's, you know.
Max. He's got girls his own age
all over him, and he's got Megan.
I'm just saying, you need to open
yourself up to other possibilities."

"Got it, Mother."

Angie huffs. "You are so pissy sometimes,
you know that?"

She stalks off.
I rip into class,

ready to plunge my hand into some clay,
pretend it's Angie's mouth,
and I am mashing it, mashing it shut.

But today,
we are doing string art.

Maybe I could make a noose
and hang her.

Cry Me a River

Waiting for the bus,
Angie picks at a scab on her elbow.
"God, look at this.
It's disgusting.
I'm never going Rollerblading again."

"Hey, what are you guys doing Saturday?"
Rachel asks,
trying to ignore the tension
that sits like an elephant between Angie and me.
I know I should say something,
make a joke,
something witty like,
"Yeah, scabby elbows suck.
That's why I got rid of my arm."

But I don't feel like being the glue.
To hell with being glue, as a matter of fact.
Angie should be more aware.
She doesn't look at me
as we board the bus.

She knows I'm right.

Letter from Barry Epson,
VP of Inspire Publishing

Dear Ms. Arrowood:

I am shocked and saddened by what has happened to you, and I send my deepest sympathy for your loss.

I am sure your recovery will be long, but I wonder if you will find this all makes you stronger in a way. It is my personal experience that sharing your story with others can help in the healing process. Which is why I am writing today. Ms. Arrowood, we would so love to interview you for our series, "American Inspirations." In case you haven't seen it, this is a weekly feature in our magazine about Americans who have overcome huge obstacles in their lives and gone on to triumph. I am sure your story would be inspirational and powerful, and who knows? You may very well help someone else who is suffering, too.

Please contact me at your earliest convenience. I sincerely hope you will say yes.

Best wishes,

Barry Epson

It Occurs to Me

Mom could have
tucked away
my pencils,
my bottles of nail polish,
the ball of half-knit yarn
before I came home from the hospital.

Did she stand in my room,
and wonder if she should?
I think
she must have.
She's that kind of wonderer.

But she left it as it was.

I look over at her on the couch,
watching TV.

I'd like to thank her,
but I'm not sure how.

Emily Morrison

Emily bumps her tray into mine
as we negotiate the
cafeteria line.
She gives me a look
that could wilt lettuce.

Eating, listening to Angie
give me mascara advice,
I think about Emily and the girls
around here,
the popular ones. Boys, too.

They want to flatten everyone
all the time.
Anyone who challenges
their own feelings of self-worth.

"When someone is jealous of you,
they make themselves your enemy."
That's what Uncle Ben told me once.

But I'm Shark Girl.
Why would anyone be jealous
of *me*?

So Angie Was Right

He glances over,
but he's too busy talking
to Megan Dalloway
to really see me.

I stand there,
ridiculous in the wake of
Megan's long, sleek hair, perky nose,
and slim, perfect body.

You know the part in Cinderella
when everyone goes to the ball
and she sits at home, crying?
It wasn't because her gown was ripped.
It was because she knew
she was an idiot
for thinking
she could grab a prince.

I know how she feels.

Blowup

"Jane, I have to tell you,
red is not your color.
You wear too much of it."
In the cafeteria,
chewing around a stick of celery,
Angie announces this in front of my friends.
"It makes you look kind of,
I don't know. Pale."

"Since when are you my fashion consultant?"
I say. I've had it. "Who asked you?
Who the hell do you think you are?
Stop picking on me, Angie! Just STOP!"
Tears burst out, run down my cheeks.
I run out of there like a baby.
Crying in the restroom.
Trying to erase Angie's stunned face,
Rachel's stricken stare,
the jeering "Tell the bitch,"
from Emily Morrison
as I ran past.

Angie knows she's hurting me
when she talks like that,
and she doesn't care.

We're through.

Letter from Naomi,
Northern California

Dear Jane,

  I can't believe what happened to you. My friend's dad is a doctor. He says losing an arm is way worse than losing a leg. I hope you're feeling better.

  Get well soon!

  Your friend,

  Naomi

Phone Call, May 1

"Are you guys going to be mad at each other forever? Is this it?"

"I don't know."

"Jane, you can't let this break up our group."

"I know. I'm the glue."

"What?"

"Nothing."

"Come on, Jane, you're bigger than this. You're pouting."

"Whose side are you on?"

"I refuse to take sides, that's just it. You guys are dividing the group. Elizabeth and Trina don't know what to do."

"You know what she's like. Why doesn't she just come right out and say it? I'm hideous. 'Jane, you really should camouflage that deformity you've got. Wear more makeup. Grow your hair into a cloak and wrap yourself in it.' I hate her."

"You're being stubborn. And you really hurt her feelings."

"You're taking sides."

"I am NOT. But she is just trying to help, in her own screwed up, kind of shallow way."

"She says the most stupid things. It's like she doesn't even think about what I'm going through."

"Jane. Angie was like that *before* your accident. And we *all* try to think about what you're going through. Since last summer, we've tried so hard. We're only human."

"Meaning?"

"You're not the only one with feelings."

"I know that!"

"She's really upset, Jane. Please talk to her. Just think about it, okay?"

"Maybe."

"I have to tell you. That surprise birthday party we threw for you? It was Angie's idea."

"No."

"Yeah. She wanted to do something special for you. She said you had been through so much and you deserved to be treated really special."

"Angie?"

"You know she can be nice! Think about it, okay?"

"Why did you have to tell me that? Now I feel rotten."

"I can think of a cure for that."

"Don't rush me."

"Think about it."

Monday

Max pulls up
as we stand outside school,
waiting for our buses.
"Jane, need a ride home?"

Rachel gives me a fierce poke.
"Call me later," she whispers.
Elizabeth gives me the wide-eyed "Wow" look.
Angie, standing apart from us,
watches silently.

Driving,
Max and I talk and talk.
I wish
all the traffic lights
would stay red.

Spring

I check with Lindsey
to see if I can plan
a party for the kids at the hospital.
Something, *some* reason
for them to all have some fun.
Lindsey says,
"We are way ahead of you, babe.
Our spring party is on the twenty-third."
"Oh. Good," I say.
"We'd sure love to have you
come help," Lindsey says.
"We could use some help decorating,
face painting,
and serving food."
She is grinning as she fills out papers.
"You're welcome to bring a date,
if you'd like.
Do you have someone to bring?"

Should I invite him?
People may talk.
He may say no. But

what the hell? Smiling, I answer her.
"Actually, I know just who to ask."

Finished, I Think

Well.
There it is.
We'll see what Justin thinks
of his present.
I think about showing Mom,
or Michael,
then decide not to. It is for Justin,
only.
Wrapped up tight in red paper,
I slide the thing deep into my closet,
then close the door.

Suppose

Suppose he hates it?

Are we doing this again? I'm trying to sleep. Besides, he won't hate it.

You're not showing it to anyone because you know what their reaction will be. Pity. Sadness. Suppose they stop push-ing you and admit it. You may never draw well again.

Stop.

Suppose this had never happened. You wouldn't even have this problem. You wouldn't even know Justin and you wouldn't have this birthday to worry about.

It's not a worry.

Suppose you had stayed home that day instead of going to the beach? It could have been different.

I cannot keep thinking like this. I won't.

It should have been different.

But it's not.

Different.

An E-Mail from Michael, May 9

Did you know UCLA has
an awesome school of occupational therapy?

(I did.)

I'll bring the lit. home this summer.

(I've got it.)

Not that I want you going here while I'm
here, J-Pain.

Hey, Mother's Day is coming. I think you
should make Mom those lemon bar things like
you always do. You know they're her
favorite.

(His, too.)

And if you want, you could make extra,
and send some here.

M.

Lemon Bars

Mabel hovers,
licking up spilled sugar, salt.
I do the mixing, dropping, picking up,
and pouring
without tears, without bad language,
even when I'm tempted.

The bars come out with
a crispy crust,
a tart, golden filling,
smelling sweet
and light.

I come out with
flour in my hair,
burned thumb throbbing,
dishes to wash, a slippery floor to vacuum.
"Lemon bar things"
are a real pain.

But then again, Mom is worth it.

I set some aside for Michael, in a box.
Getting to the post office will be a pain.

But then again,
he saved my life.

Mother's Day

Mom? I brought you some tea.

Mmm.

I can't believe you have the flu on Mother's Day.

Lucky me. Hey, what's that? Are those lemon bars?

Yeah. Here, sit up.

Oh, honey. You made these for me? Thank you!

You're welcome. Here's your card, and stuff.

This is all so nice. Thank you. Wow. These are great.
You haven't lost your touch.

Not entirely.

Michael will be jealous.

I've got some for him, too. I'll mail them out tomorrow.

Need me to drive you to the post office?

No, I can walk. I can handle it.

I know you can. It might be easier if I drive you.

You don't have to.

I know. I want to. Okay? I still like to do things for you, you know.

Yeah, but—

Not because of your arm or anything else. Because you're my daughter. You know? You'll always be my little girl, to some extent.

Mom, stop. Okay, you can drive me.

Thanks. Moms need to help their kids once in a while, you know. It keeps us feeling useful.

But you can only drive if you're feeling better.

I will be fine. I can't take a sick day off, anyway.

Mom, you should. Take it easy for one day, okay? The world won't fall apart.

Well, when did you get so wise? Now who's being the mom?

I'm just saying. You'd make me stay home if I were sick. Besides, you'll only infect everyone else if you go in.

That's right. You're right. You'd make a good doctor, by the way. Have I told you that?

You saw my pamphlet from the medical school.

I did. When did this happen? Are you thinking of a career in medicine now? Is that why you volunteer at the hospital?

It's just something I think about sometimes. And being at the hospital is . . . I don't know, good. It helps me think about what's important, I guess. What I want.

And what is that?

For you to get well. And eat another lemon bar.

Yes, ma'am. But Jane. I haven't seen you drawing at all. We're coming up on a year now. Do you plan on ever taking art back up again?

Yes.

That's it—"Yes"? What are you waiting for?

The right time. It's hard to explain.

Oh.

You want to watch a movie or something? I can see what's on.

Sure. And honey?

Yeah?

I'm proud of you. You've been through a lot, and you're doing great.

I'm proud of you, too, Mom. Same reason.

This calls for another lemon bar.

Hey. Save one for me.

Red Streaks

Are they fading, just a little?
In the mirror,
I study it. It's not going anywhere.
Avoiding it
hasn't proved useful.

I sprinkle on some baby powder,
touch the rounded, smooth flesh,
compare the differing thicknesses
of my two upper arms.

Somehow,
this thing
that was once alien
is returning to being
part of me.

Sparkle

This morning I opened Angie's
makeup kit, the one she gave me,
and looked through it again.

Among the purples,
there's a delicate blush,
sparkly on my cheeks,
subtle, smooth. Something
I may have actually
picked out myself.

Pride

Keeps me from walking up to her,
from saying,
"Sorry."

But it doesn't keep me from noticing
how she turns her head away,
how her eyes blink fast, how she's
pretending with her whole body
that she doesn't care
when I walk past her seat on the bus.

The Wall

We sit at lunch,
a nation divided.

The others don't know who to side with.
Angie and I,
by unspoken agreement,
sit at either end of the same table
so Rachel, Trina, and Elizabeth
can sit between us.

Nobody can actually eat.
Our throats are full
of words unsaid.

The Talk

I corner Angie on the way to the bus stop.
Trapped between the building
and the parking lot,
there is nowhere for her to run,
no crowds to melt into.
I want to lie down in the path
of an oncoming bus.
Anything but talk to her.
But I have to make this right.
"Angie, look. I just want . . ."
I steady my voice.
"I want us to be friends again. I want you to stop
being mad at me."

With the ball in her court,
Angie holds the power.
She looks down at the books in her arms
and shrugs. In a small voice, she says,
"You're just so different lately."

Yes, I AM different, I want to shout,
I want to wave my fake arm around.
Angie says, "I mean . . .
what I meant was, I *know* you're different now,
but you just seem so MAD all the time.
What did I do?"

I could list. But I say only,
"Sometimes you just get kind of bossy.
Like with my hair,
you wanted me to get your permission to cut it.
And my makeup.
This is the way I wear it.
I don't want to change.
I've changed enough."

With each excuse, I shrink.
Smaller and smaller,
until I am a marble on the sidewalk.

Such petty crap.
God, do I really think
our problems are about hair and makeup?

We're standing here crying.
Let's get to the truth, and end this.
So I dig deep, and pull out
the darkest seed I find.
"The thing you said about Max.
It really hurt my feelings."

She looks up at me.

"I need you to be on my side,"
I say.

"I am," she starts, then wilts.
There is a long silence.

"I'm sorry.
I was trying to help," Angie says,
still in a small voice.
"We're *all* just trying to help."
She shifts. "I don't want to see you get hurt again."

Now comes the question.
Do I believe her?
Because this would make an easy way out,
and then we could go back to pretending.
But looking at Angie's face,
the weird thing is,
I do believe her.
In her own way,
she wanted to make me over into someone
like her,
someone who gets guys and
who doesn't get hurt by the serious stuff
because the serious stuff
doesn't get acknowledged.

And all of this makes it easier to say

"I'm sorry, too."

Two inches shorter than me,
too thin, and her lipstick all smeared.
What was I afraid of?
She is my friend.
Not my final answer.
She can stop protecting me,
and I can help her do that.
Only nicely.

I'm going to start living again,
only differently.

When Angie looks up at me,
I think maybe, she is seeing what I just saw.
The two of us,
with everything changed.

"Can we just try again?" I ask,
and after a pause filled with the sounds
of rumbling bus engines and
students' loud voices as they crowd past us,
Angie nods.

So we walk home,
trying again.

May 23: Party on the Second Floor

"Happy Spring," Lindsey says,
squashing me close.

"Happy Spring, Lindsey."

"And let me give your date a hug," Lindsey says.
"I must say, you are a handsome fellow."
Justin grins.
He wraps his skinny arms
around Lindsey's waist.
"Happy Spring."

The kids, in bathrobes and gowns, two in
party hats,
gather in the cafeteria.
The ones that are too sick to come
will be visited later by all of us,
with toys, plates of cookies,
and most important,
understanding
and compassion.
I ache for them. But I focus on the faces
before me; eager, wanting some fun.

"Who wants their face painted?"

Old Faces and New

I left Chuck at home.
Who needs that hot thing?
I'm busy painting faces.
It's kind of a mess, but the kids don't mind.

Justin helps with the games,
nurses pass out treats,
Dr. Kim and Mel come by my table for a hug
and hello.
"It's good to see you." Dr. Kim says,
then his pager goes off.
He whips out of there, waving.

"How's it going, kiddo?" Mel says.
He plants a kiss on the top of my head.
Plops down in the chair before me.
I begin painting
a lopsided sunflower on his cheek.

"Mel?"
"Yeah?"
"Do you remember when I told you—
when I said—that—
sometimes, I wished I had died that day?"

"Yes, I do."
I dab a tiny leaf on the flower's stem.
"I don't feel that way anymore."

Mel smiles. "What changed your mind?"
I stop. I think.
A little Justin, a little Mel,
a lot of Mom and Michael,
some Rachel, some Max,
Uncle Ben and Aunt Karen,
even some Angie,
and maybe something else.
But what?

"I'm not sure."
Mel nods. "Someday, you will. For now,
enjoy the feeling."

So I do as he says,

and enjoy.

Justin's Gift

As the kids glue together
tissue-paper flowers,
and parents hold each other's hands,
I poke Justin.
"Come outside for a minute."
He steps out with me
into the hall
where it is cool and quiet.

I give him the tube I've been hiding.
"Happy Birthday."

Justin shakes out the rolled-up paper inside.
He unfurls it and

his face

splits

into

a huge

grin.

"That's her!" He shows me
the pastel sketch,

as though I didn't make it,
as though I haven't seen it.
"That's Spot!"

"Do you like it?"

Justin is still grinning at the drawing.
"It's so *good*."

"I'm still pretty wobbly. I tried
to get everything right,
but some of the colors smooshed around on me."

Justin shakes his head. "It's perfect."

Another hug,
and this time I hold on to him, tight.
I love Justin as much as I love Michael.
But

something is drawing to a close tonight,
and I know
it will be a long time
before I see Justin again.
We're moving on with our lives.
He has his friends, his family, his life,
and I have mine.

It's time to let go.

Memorial

Company is coming for dinner.
Two of Mom's teacher friends
who play a mean game of croquet.
Angie, Rachel, Elizabeth, and Trina
are due to arrive any second.
Aunt Karen and Uncle Ben, visiting
for the weekend, fuss with their
matching dress shirts.
Michael wears shorts that are not ripped.
That's his idea of dressed up.
Mom looks beautiful in her red tank
and shimmery skirt.
I have painted my toenails in honor
of the occasion:
our annual Memorial Day cookout.
A kickoff to summer.

"Did you ever see a nicer-looking bunch?" Mom asks,
and Michael smiles, gathering up
fork, spatula, and timer
for the grill.
"Mom, you say that every year."

Mom picks up her camera.
"Well, this year . . ."

"—*I really mean it,*" Michael and I chant in unison,
turning to her to make a face,
and when we both laugh,
Mom snaps a picture.

Done

If only you had helped that woman. If only you had—

Shut up.

You lost your arm.

Yeah, I noticed. Now shut up.

You—

I'm done doing this to myself. Got it? Done.

But it could have been different—

It wasn't. It is what it is. And yeah, it sucks. But listening to this crap doesn't help.

But—

It doesn't help. I'm done.

It—

Done.

Not Knowing

At the albums again,
open pages, shiny plastic,
shielding us,
the Old Us,
spread out in photos,
a time line
of our innocence.

Dad: lighting the grill,
holding back my small hand
as I reach for the flame;
he is free
from the knowledge
that soon
he will be dead from cancer.

Mom, posing before her new car,
Michael clinging to her leg,
me, barely more than a lump,
lying across her arms.
She had no idea
that soon, she would be left
to raise us
by herself.

None of us knew.
None of us know now.